06.

THE VÁSQUEZ
MISTRESS

THE VÁSQUEZ MISTRESS

BY

SARAH MORGAN

MILLS & BOON®
Pure reading pleasure™

First published in Great Britain 2008
Large Print edition 2009
Harlequin Mills & Boon Limited,
Eton House, 18-24 Paradise Road,
Richmond, Surrey TW9 1SR

© Sarah Morgan 2008

ISBN: 978 0 263 20564 0

Set in Times Roman 16½ on 18½ pt.
16-0209-55446

Printed and bound in Great Britain
by CPI Antony Rowe, Chippenham, Wiltshire

CHAPTER ONE

SHE sat straight as a warrior on the horse, her hair gleaming like liquid gold under the baking Argentine sun.

When he'd first noticed her in the distance his reaction had been one of irritation, partly because the horse had been galloping hard in the ferocious heat, but mostly because he'd been seeking solitude, not company. And if there was one thing that the Argentine pampas offered in abundance it was the opportunity for solitude.

Endless grassland stretched far into the distance, the horizon so perfectly straight and flat that it might have been drawn with a ruler.

Irritation had turned to concern as horse and rider had drawn closer and he'd recognised the animal she was riding.

He felt a flash of anger towards whomever had allowed her to take that particular horse out alone and made a mental note to find the culprit.

And then anger faded to slow, simmering masculine appraisal as he scanned the delicate lines of her features.

He had spent his life surrounded by exceptionally beautiful women, all of them more groomed than this girl, and yet he couldn't drag his eyes away from her face. She was fair-skinned and delicate, her body a mouth-watering combination of slender limbs and perfect curves. It was as if she'd been created by the gods and thrown onto Earth for the simple purpose of tempting man.

Her creamy skin and flushed cheeks gave her an air of innocence and he gave a wry smile, surprised that he was even capable of recognising that particular quality given how rarely he'd met with it before.

In fact his cynicism was so deep-rooted that his first thought when he'd noticed her on the horizon had been to assume that she'd somehow tracked him down and followed him. But he'd dismissed that possibility instantly, knowing that her presence could only be coincidence.

A happy coincidence, he thought idly, his eyes resting on her soft mouth. A very happy coincidence indeed.

* * *

The horse flattened his ears, arched his back and gave a ferocious buck that should have unseated her.

Faith gritted her teeth and managed to stay glued to the saddle. 'You really are in a horrible mood today, Fuego. It's no wonder everyone is afraid of you,' she muttered. 'I'm not falling off here. We're miles from home. Wherever you go, I go and the sooner you realise that the better for both of us.'

The heat was stifling and she reached for her bottle of water and then froze as she caught movement out of the corner of her eye. She turned her head, the breath jamming in her throat as she saw a man watching her.

She'd been concentrating so hard on not falling off the horse, that she hadn't noticed him.

But she noticed him now.

He was the most staggeringly handsome man she'd ever met and since she'd arrived in Argentina, she'd met quite a few. His body was lean and hard, his shoulders broad and powerful but what really disrupted the steady rhythm of her heart was the sheer raw sexuality that surrounded him like a forcefield.

'You're staring, *signorina*.' His deep, male

voice trickled through her veins like a drug and her limbs weakened.

Her horse, sensing a lack of concentration on her part, chose that moment to give another determined buck and Faith flew into the air and landed on her bottom in the dust.

'For crying out loud!' Pain shot through her and she sat for a moment, working out whether anything was broken. 'That horse needs a psychiatrist.'

A pair of strong male hands closed around her waist and lifted her easily to her feet. 'He needs a male rider.' His eyes blazed fiercely into hers and she felt her heart stumble and trip.

'There's nothing wrong with my riding. It's your fault for jumping out on me with no warning…' Her voice tailed off because the sudden narrowing of his beautiful, sexy eyes drove all thoughts from her head.

'I assumed you'd seen me. The Argentine grassland hardly offers a large number of hiding places.'

'I was concentrating on my horse.'

'You were riding too fast.'

'Tell that to the horse, not me. I suppose that's why they called him Fuego—my Spanish isn't great, but I know it means "fire".' Faith dragged her gaze away from his handsome face in the hope that not looking at him might help her slow the crazy beating of her heart. 'I didn't choose the pace. With that particular horse, you always get more than you bargain for.' *What was the matter with her?* She felt light-headed and dizzy and her body felt alarmingly lethargic.

It was the heat, she told herself quickly. Just the relentless, baking heat that turned the entire landscape into a throbbing, sultry outdoor sauna.

'You are staying at the Estancia La Lucia?' He glanced behind him even though the elegant colonial house was over an hour away. 'You shouldn't be riding alone. What happened to the rest of your party? You should have a groom with you.'

'Oh, please.' Baking hot from the relentless sunshine and aching from her fall, Faith shot him a warning look. 'I'm just not in the mood for all that macho Argentine-man thing. Not right now.'

He lifted an eyebrow in silent mockery. 'Argentine-man thing?'

'You know what I mean.' She rubbed at the dirt on her breeches. 'The mega-macho approach.

The "sling a woman over your shoulder" method of communication.'

'Interesting description.' His eyes laughed into hers. 'This is South America, *cariño*. Men know how to be men.'

'I'd noticed. Ever since I stepped off the aeroplane I've been surrounded by so much testosterone that it's driving me mad.'

'Welcome to Argentina.' There was gentle mockery in his sexy, accented drawl and suddenly she felt impossibly awkward and shy and her reaction to him infuriated her because she'd always thought of herself as a confident person.

'Do you work here?'

His hesitation was so brief she decided that she must have imagined it. 'Yes.'

'Lucky you.' She assumed he must be one of the *gauchos*, the cowboys who worked with the nine-hundred head of cattle that grazed this land. Dragging her eyes away from his, she wondered why this particular man was having such an effect on her. Yes, he was good-looking but so were many of the men she'd met since she'd arrived in South America.

But there was something about him…

'Your English is amazing.'

'That's because I sometimes talk to women before I throw them over my shoulder.' He studied her for a long disturbing moment, a powerful, confident male totally at home in his surroundings. Then his gaze dropped to her mouth and lingered there, as if he were making up his mind about something.

The heat went from oppressive to unbearable and the chemistry between them was so shockingly intense that she actually felt herself sway towards him in anticipation.

She *desperately* wanted him to kiss her and the strength of that need shocked her because she'd been pushing men away since the day she'd arrived at Buenos Aires. She was here to work, study and learn, not to meet a man. But suddenly her lips were tingling with anticipation and she found herself trapped by the lazy, knowing expression in his dangerously attractive eyes. It was as if he was savouring the moment and she knew that he'd read her thoughts. Her sense of anticipation exploded into an all-consuming sexual excitement that she'd never before experienced.

She waited breathlessly, knowing that she was poised on the brink of something wickedly exciting and sensing that this man was going to change her life for ever.

But instead of kissing her he gave a slow, expressive smile and turned his attention to her horse. 'Your horse needs a drink.'

Released from the force of his gaze, Faith felt her entire body go limp and her face flood with colour. 'My horse needs a lot of things.'

What had happened just then?

Had she imagined the connection between them? Had it all been in her head?

Her eyes slid to his broad shoulders and the long, lean length of his strong legs as he led her horse to the river.

No, she hadn't imagined it. But this was no teenage boy eager for a quick grope and instant satisfaction; she was dealing with someone else entirely. He was all man, from the glossy black hair and darkened jaw to the powerful muscle that hardened his unmistakably male physique. He was cool, sophisticated and experienced and her stomach curled inside her because he carried himself with such confidence and she knew, she just *knew*, that he was playing with her.

Feeling as though the temperature had just shot up by a hundred degrees, Faith glared at his broad back and then bit her lip, wishing she could get rid of the agonising sizzle that was burning inside her.

Angry with herself *and* with him, she lifted her chin and strolled towards him, determined not to let him see how much he'd affected her.

'I need to be getting back.' She took Fuego's reins and vaulted into the saddle, taking some satisfaction from the way the man's eyes lingered on her slim thighs.

She hadn't imagined the chemistry. *The searing attraction wasn't all on her side.*

'Wait.' He closed a hand over Fuego's reins, preventing the horse from moving. 'You say that you work at the *estancia*. In what capacity? Do you work in the guest quarters?'

'You're showing your prejudices again.' Agonisingly aware of him, she rubbed a hand over the horse's neck to focus herself. 'All the Argentine men I've met so far seem to think that a woman's place is in the—' She stopped herself just in time, but he lifted an eyebrow, his eyes gleaming with wicked humour.

'You were saying? We Argentine men think a woman's place is in the…?'

He was so desperately attractive that for a

moment she couldn't speak and she certainly didn't want to finish her sentence. It would draw the conversation towards an extremely dangerous area that she knew was best avoided. 'Kitchen,' she said lamely. 'Kitchen.'

His smile deepened. 'Kitchen? If that's what you think then you obviously haven't yet deciphered the workings of the average male mind here in South America.'

That smile connected straight to her nerve endings and she was infuriated with herself for being so susceptible to his charm and masculinity.

'The average male mind is of absolutely no interest to me,' she said sweetly, 'unless the mind belongs to a horse.'

'Is that what brought you to Argentina? Our horses?'

Faith glanced around her, at the endless sweep of grassland that surrounded them. 'I came because I read about Raul Vásquez.'

The man stilled. 'You travelled thousands of miles to meet Raul Vásquez?' There was a coolness to his tone that had been absent before. 'You are hoping to catch yourself a billionaire, perhaps?'

Faith gazed at him in astonishment and then burst out laughing. 'No, of course not. Don't be ridiculous. Billionaire polo-patrons aren't exactly my style, and anyway, I've never even met the man. He's off in the States at the moment, negotiating some high-flying deal or other and he employs thousands of people. I don't expect our paths are ever going to cross.'

He studied her with disturbing intensity. 'And that would disappoint you?'

'You misunderstand me. I'm not interested in the man, but I *am* interested in his polo *estancia*. That's why I'm here. Raul Vásquez breeds horses and trains them and his vet facilities are the best in the world. I read a paper in a journal written by Eduardo, his chief vet. I contacted him. Landing a job here is my dream come true.'

'Eduardo employed you?' That statement was greeted by incredulous silence. 'You're a *vet*?'

'Yes, I'm a vet.' Watching the frank astonishment in his eyes, Faith gritted her teeth. 'Welcome to the twenty-first century. Women do become vets, you know. Some of us can even walk and talk at the same time, although news of that accomplishment clearly hasn't yet reached South America.'

'I'm aware that some women become vets,' he said smoothly, 'But this is a busy, commercial stud-farm, not some small-animal practice in the city.'

'I wasn't interested in a small-animal practice. For me it's always been about horses.'

His gaze slid to her arms and lingered. 'I don't doubt your commitment or your enthusiasm, but sometimes physical strength is required, especially out here in the pampas where we deal with powerful stallions and hormonal mares.'

Her heart rate suddenly doubled. 'Here we go again. You think it's all about muscle, aggression and domination, but what you need to realise is that there's more to horsemanship than brute strength. And Raul Vásquez understands that. He has some revolutionary training methods.'

'I'm fully aware of his training methods. Answer me one question...' His tone was soft and deadly and his gaze returned to her face. 'Who was in charge when you were galloping across the pampas with the wind in your hair? You or the horse?'

'Oh, the horse,' Faith admitted, her eyes sparkling with humour. 'But brute force wouldn't have changed that fact.'

'He needs to be ridden by a man. A man with sufficient skill and strength to control him.'

Faith came back at him instantly. 'He needs to be understood. If you want to change behaviour, then you have to first try and understand the reason behind that behaviour. Horses do things for a reason, just like humans.'

She'd spent her life studying and all her spare time around horses. No man had ever captured her attention.

Until now.

His confidence and sophistication tied her in knots and she felt horribly self-conscious and more than a little confused by her own reaction.

She would never in a million years have described herself as shy, but suddenly she was agonisingly aware of her own naivety when it came to men like him.

'I'd better be going. I have to ride back and…' Her voice tailed off and she wondered whether he was going to stop her.

But he didn't.

He let his hand drop from Fuego's bridle and stepped away. 'Ride carefully,' he said softly and she gave a puzzled smile because she'd been so, so sure that he was going to stop her or at least suggest that they meet again.

And she'd wanted him to.

She'd really wanted him to.

* * *

The Vásquez Polo Cup was an important annual part of the Argentine polo circuit and it was the most glittering, glamorous affair Faith had ever attended.

She was only there in her official capacity as a vet of course, but she couldn't help glancing towards the spectators who were gathering in the stands. 'How come the women are all so stunning?' she wondered out loud. 'And how do they achieve such straight hair? In this heat my hair just curls.'

'You are looking at the elite of Buenos Aires,' Eduardo replied, breaking off to shout instructions to one of the grooms before turning his attention back to Faith. 'They would have spent the whole of the day preparing in the hope that they catch the boss's eye.'

'The boss?' Faith glanced around her. 'Raul Vásquez? He's playing today isn't he? Is he here?'

'Not yet.'

'But the game is due to start in five minutes.' She couldn't take her eyes off the women in the stands, her attention caught by the glint of diamonds against designer silk. They were like a flock of exotic birds. 'They're very dressed up considering they're spending their afternoon around horses.'

'This is polo,' Eduardo drawled. 'The most glamorous game in the world. Everyone dresses up.'

The men thundered onto the field on lithe, agile horses and Faith tried not to be overwhelmed by the sheer glamour of the spectacle.

She'd just stooped to examine a horse's fetlock when she heard the noise of a helicopter in the air.

'Here he comes,' Eduardo murmured, glancing upwards and narrowing his eyes against the glare of the sun. 'Match starts in two minutes. He's cutting it fine as usual.'

Faith was too busy with the pony to pay any attention to the helicopter landing. 'He isn't fit.'

Eduardo frowned. 'He's the fittest man I've ever met.'

'Not the boss, this pony!' Faith stared at him in exasperation. 'Does everyone here only think about Raul Vásquez?'

There was a sudden roar from the crowd and Faith realised that the game had started. She glanced over her shoulder, watching as horses and riders thundered down the pitch.

Before arriving in Argentina she'd never been

to a polo match and the speed and danger of the game still left her breathless.

She turned to one of the grooms. 'Which one is Raul Vásquez?'

'The one taking all the risks,' he muttered and Faith's eyes narrowed as she turned her attention to the game.

From this distance it was impossible to distinguish anyone's features under the protective helmet, but one man stood out from all the others. Lithe and muscular, he controlled his horse with one hand while he leaned out of the saddle to hook the ball, apparently indifferent to the danger inherent in such a manoeuvre.

Watching in disbelief, Faith braced herself for him to crash to the ground with disastrous consequences. He had to fall, surely? But with a mixture of sheer muscle-strength and athleticism, he stayed with the horse, swung his mallet with lethal accuracy and hit the ball through the posts.

The crowd erupted in ecstasy and Faith suddenly realised that she'd been holding her breath.

'The tension of this game is unbelievable,' she muttered and the groom grinned at her.

'It is very aggressive, yes. But the horses love it.'

Turning her attention back to her job, Faith worked her way down the pony lines, checking each animal and talking to the grooms, and at half time one of the grooms tapped her on the shoulder. 'Time to stomp the divets. It's tradition. Everyone joins in.'

Spectators and players strolled onto the pitch and started treading in the lumps of turf that had been dislodged by the horses' hooves. It was a social occasion, with much laughter and conversation, a chance for the audience to mingle with the players.

Faith stretched out her foot to push down a lump of grass but a large black boot was there before her and she glanced up into the laughing eyes of the man she'd been watching on the polo field.

Raul Vásquez.

The man from the river.

For a moment she just stared. Then she swallowed and her tongue seemed to tie itself into knots. 'I didn't know. You didn't introduce yourself.'

'I didn't want to,' he drawled softly and hot colour flooded her cheeks because he was just so, *so* attractive and although they were surrounded by beautiful, glamorous women, he was looking at *her*.

'You should have told me who you were!'

'Why? You might have behaved differently and I wouldn't have wanted that.' His smile was sexy, distracting and impossibly intimate.

'How did I behave?'

He stamped down another piece of turf and his leg brushed against hers in a deliberate movement. 'You were delightfully natural.'

She glanced around her at the poise and confidence of the women around her. 'You mean I don't spend all day being pampered. Why are you talking to me?'

'Because you fascinate me.'

'You prefer your women with no make-up and covered in dust?'

He laughed. 'I'm interested in the person, not the package.'

'Oh please!' She stared up at his impossibly handsome face. 'Are you seriously telling me that you would look twice at a woman who wasn't stunning?'

'No, I'm not telling you that.' His eyes didn't leave hers and she felt as if the air had been knocked out of her lungs.

'You're saying that—you're implying that—'

'Yes.' His tone was amused. 'I am. And you're not usually short of a sharp reply. What's the matter? Hasn't anyone paid you a compliment before?'

The chemistry between them crackled and sizzled like a high-voltage cable and she was conscious of what seemed like hundreds of eyes looking at her. 'Everyone is staring.'

'And that matters because…?'

'Well, you might be used to being the centre of attention, but I'm not.' Not knowing what to say and frustrated with herself for being so gauche, she glared at him. 'It doesn't matter who you are, I still think you're macho and sexist.'

He threw his head back and laughed. 'You're absolutely right, *cariño*. I am macho and sexist. And I want to spend some time with you. Come to the Beach House.'

The Beach House was his private residence, a beautiful architect-designed villa that faced the Atlantic coast and opened onto a perfect stretch of sand. And it was strictly out of bounds to the staff.

What exactly was he suggesting?

But one glance at his wicked dark eyes told her

exactly what he was suggesting and the colour rushed into her cheeks like fire.

Unsettled by how much she wanted to say yes, Faith stepped away, conscious that all the women on the pitch were watching her enviously. How on earth was she supposed to say no to a man like him? Worried that part of her didn't even want to say no, she spoke quickly before she could be tempted into doing something she just knew she'd regret. 'No. But thanks.'

'I wasn't asking you a question.'

She was suddenly so aware of him that her entire body was burning inside. 'You were giving me an order?'

His gaze was lazily amused. 'A strongly worded request.'

She could hardly breathe. 'I have a job to do. I'm working until ten.'

'I'll arrange for you to have the evening off.'

Just like that.

The power of a billionaire, Faith thought helplessly. 'No. That wouldn't be fair on the others.' She was swamped with disappointment and suddenly wondered what she would have said if she *hadn't* been working. Would she have gone with him? Her insides fluttered with nerves. 'I'm afraid we're going to have to postpone my Cinderella moment for another occasion. It's Eduardo's night off and we have a mare due to foal any minute. I can't leave the yard.'

The humour died in his eyes and her words were met by a tense silence. 'One of the mares is due to foal?' Easy seduction was replaced by sharp efficiency. 'Which one?'

'Velocity.'

He inhaled sharply and ran a hand over the back of his neck. 'If she is foaling then Eduardo should be here.' His cool declaration punctured her bubble of happiness.

'Well, thanks for that vote of confidence. Nice to know you trust me.'

'It isn't personal.'

She gave a short laugh. 'You mean you'd feel like this about any woman?'

His eyes narrowed dangerously. 'Velocity is my most valuable mare. This is an enormous responsibility,' he said softly, and she lifted her chin and looked him straight in the eye.

'I can handle responsibility. I don't spend my days straightening my hair and applying my make-up. I've trained for seven years so that I can meet the responsibility head-on.' Suddenly she felt angry and frustrated. Maybe she'd been wrong to think she could pursue her career in this part of South America. It was an uphill battle to get anyone to take her seriously. 'I can handle the work. What I can't handle is dealing with men who don't think women are capable of having a career.' She was so upset she was afraid she might burst into tears. *And that would undermine her credibility even further.* 'If you'll excuse me, I have work to do.'

Trying not to think about Raul Vásquez, she worked in the stables until ten. Then she went to check on the mare, Velocity, one more time before returning to her room in the staff quarters.

A single glance was sufficient for her to see that the mare was in difficulty.

The groom was in the corner of the stall, his hands shaking as he fumbled with his mobile phone. 'I can't get hold of Eduardo. He isn't answering.'

'You should have called *me*, not Eduardo.' Faith dropped to her knees beside the horse. Cursing herself for relying on them to let her know how the mare was progressing, she reached for her stethoscope.

The groom was sweating. 'You better not touch that horse. She's the boss's favourite mare. If anything happens to her…' He broke off, panic in his eyes. 'We need to get hold of Eduardo somehow. If anything happens to the animal, Raul Vásquez will hit the roof. I'll lose my job.'

Faith gritted her teeth. *None of the Argentine grooms had faith in her.*

'At the moment I don't care about the boss's temper or your promotion prospects, but I *do* care about the horse and you need to do as I tell you.' Keeping her voice calm so it didn't disturb the animal, Faith gave him a string of instructions but he just stood there, staring at the horse with terrified eyes.

'If that mare dies—'

'It will be my responsibility,' Faith said coldly and then she sighed. 'Oh for goodness' sake, just get out. If you can't work with me, fine, but I need you to find someone who *can*. I need help and I need it now.'

'I will help you.' Raul Vásquez stood in the doorway of the box and the groom shrank into the shadows, too intimidated to even defend himself.

Faith was too worried about the mare to feel intimidated. With barely a glance in his direction, she told Raul what she wanted him to do and he immediately dropped to his haunches next to the mare and spoke to her softly in Spanish.

Faith had no idea what he said but his words had an immediate effect on the frightened animal and finally she was able to concentrate, which was just as well because it was the most difficult foaling she'd ever attended.

Finally the mare heaved a sigh and the foal slipped out onto the straw.

'Clever girl,' Faith breathed quietly and glanced up, suddenly aware that Raul was watching her intently.

'I think *you* are the clever girl,' he murmured quietly, a thoughtful expression in his dark eyes as he scanned her face with disturbing intensity. 'I underestimated you and for that I apologise.'

The atmosphere in the box was charged with tension and for a moment they just stared at each other. Then she suddenly realised that he was wearing a dinner jacket. 'I'm sorry I interrupted your evening,' she said stiffly, hating herself for caring that he'd clearly found another woman with whom to spend his evening.

It could have been her.

Remembering the sleek, beautifully groomed

women who had vied for his attention during the polo match, Faith wondered which of them had caught his attention. Then she gave herself a mental shake. It could *never* have been her. Men as rich, successful and handsome as Raul Vásquez wanted trophy women, not career women.

Descending back to earth with a bump, she gave a tired smile. 'Your mare is going to be fine, Raul, but I'll stay with her tonight just to make sure. Thanks for your help. It made all the difference.'

'You are planning to sleep in my horse's stall?' At some point he had undone his top button and she caught a glimpse of bronzed male skin and a hint of curling dark hair.

'Yes.' Faith looked away quickly. *He was impossibly masculine.* 'That way if anything happens, I'll be here.'

He frowned sharply. 'You have been working since six this morning.'

'I'll take tomorrow off. I don't want to leave until I'm sure she's all right.' Her attention was back on the mare and her foal. 'You should understand that. From what I've heard, you're the original workaholic.'

'That is different.'

'Because you're a man and I'm a woman? Don't start that again, Raul.' Suddenly exhausted, she just wanted him to leave so that she could stop dreaming. 'I won't leave halfway through a job. And you were obviously in the middle of dinner or something, so perhaps you'd better go back to the woman in question in case she gives up on you.'

There was a long silence. 'You hide behind your job, don't you?' Raul asserted. 'Why is that?'

'I don't hide. But I love my job, if that's what you're asking.' She glanced at him briefly and then looked away again, her heart thumping and her mind spinning fairy-tales.

'This thing between us—' his voice was soft '—it frightens you, doesn't it?'

She was too honest to pretend she didn't know what he was talking about. 'Yes, it frightens me. Because it's not real. The mere idea of you and I is—' She waved a hand. 'It's crazy. I mean, we couldn't be more different. You're used to women who spend all day making themselves beautiful. I'm a working girl. I love my career and I definitely don't want a relationship.'

'If you don't want a relationship, then you are

my perfect woman,' he drawled softly. 'What about fun, *cariño*? Do you object to having fun?'

The colour poured into her cheeks. 'Raul—'

'Why are you blushing? When it comes to your job you are supremely confident, but whenever we are alone...' He stroked a leisurely finger down her cheek. 'Why is it that you are so confident with my horses and so shy with me?'

'Blame it on the testosterone again. I'm not used to macho men.' She tried to make a joke, but he wasn't smiling. Instead his gaze was curiously intent.

'You are very inexperienced, aren't you?'

'I've had boyfriends,' she muttered defensively and a smile played around his firm mouth.

'But what about *men*, *cariño*? Men are a whole new experience for you, isn't that right?'

She gazed at him, her heart pounding and her mouth dry. 'What does *"cariño"* mean?'

His smile widened and he strolled towards the door. 'I'll teach you tomorrow,' he answered softly. 'Along with the facts of life. Finish your job and get some rest. You're going to need it.'

CHAPTER TWO

SHE spent the night with the mare and emerged from the box to find Raul Vásquez in conversation with Eduardo.

Raul turned his head and looked at her and the look of blatant masculine appreciation in his dark eyes made her stomach flip. 'You are now officially off duty and you're coming with me.' He took her hand firmly in his, said something in Spanish to Eduardo and led her towards the helicopter pad at the far side of the polo fields.

'I was going to bed,' she mumbled and he flashed her a smile of such devastating charisma that for a moment she was blinded.

'That can be arranged.'

She didn't know whether to laugh or gasp with shock. 'I really don't do this sort of thing—'

'What sort of thing?' His eyes teased her and she glanced at the sleek lines of the black helicopter and then back over her shoulder towards the safety of the *estancia*.

'I don't fly off into the sunset with men I don't know.'

'You can spend your day sleeping in your room and then you can eat dinner with the grooms, if that is what you would prefer.' He paused and his gaze drifted to her mouth. 'Or you can have dinner with me.'

She licked her lips. 'Where?'

'Somewhere we can talk without disturbance.' He opened the door of the helicopter and she scrambled inside, wondering what on earth she was doing.

This wasn't her life.

She didn't climb into helicopters with dangerous billionaires.

While she was wrestling with self-doubt and nerves, Raul settled himself in the seat next to her and flicked several switches with swift, confident fingers.

Faith stared at him. '*You're* flying it?'

'I'm a control freak,' he confessed in a dry tone. 'I prefer to be in the driving seat and anyway, for what I have in mind, I don't need an audience.'

His words sent a shiver of anticipation

through her body. 'I don't know why you're doing this. And I don't know why I'm doing this either.' She licked her lips. 'I don't own a silk dress or diamonds.'

'Then we'll have to do something about that.' He turned towards her and there was laughter in his wicked dark eyes. 'Relax.' His voice was surprisingly gentle. 'You're going to have a nice time. This is my thank-you for saving my horse and my apology for not having more faith in you. You were impressive.'

His praise was as surprising as it was welcome. 'Your groom didn't think so. Perhaps you could have a word with him.'

'That won't be necessary. He no longer works for me.'

'You fired him?' She was shocked. 'Isn't that a little extreme?'

'You asked for his help. He didn't give it.'

Faith felt a flash of guilt. 'I didn't mean to get him fired. Shouldn't you give him another chance?'

'I gave him one chance. I employed him.' His smile didn't falter but there was something in his eyes that hinted at a more ruthless side of him. *The side that had made him a billionaire by the time he was thirty.*

Sensing that the subject was best dropped, Faith glanced around her. 'Where are we going?'

'You'll find out.' Without answering her question, he turned his attention back to the controls and the helicopter lifted into the air.

Terror soon turned to exhilaration as they swooped above the pampas. 'The view is amazing from up here,' she breathed, her eyes fixed on the landscape beneath her.

They flew over grassland, interspersed with lagoons and wetlands. Occasionally Faith saw cattle being herded by men on horseback, but this was a vast landscape and the sheer size of it took her breath away.

Eventually a large lake came into view and Raul landed the helicopter.

'We're here. This is the boundary of the *estancia*.' He jumped down from the helicopter and led her towards a luxurious lodge that nestled between water and trees. 'My secret hideaway.'

Faith stopped dead, her heart bumping against her chest. 'We're alone here?'

He turned, his eyes on her face. 'Does that bother you? Are you nervous?'

She swallowed. 'Maybe. Just a little.'

'You were alone with me on the pampas on that

first day,' he said softly, strolling back towards her and taking her face in his hands. 'And you weren't nervous then.'

'That was an accidental meeting.' The skilled brush of his fingers set her pulse racing and nerves fluttered like butterflies in her stomach. 'I don't do this sort of thing, Raul. I shouldn't have come.'

'Stop panicking. You haven't done anything yet,' he pointed out gently. 'And you won't be doing anything you don't want to. All I ask is that you allow yourself to be spoiled. This is a thank-you for having saved my favourite horse. Treat it like a spa day.'

'A spa day?'

His mouth hovered tantalisingly close to hers and then he stepped away and smiled. 'I want to spoil you. And we're not alone here. You can shout for help any time you feel the need and a hoard of staff will come running and beat me away with sticks.'

He led her up a few steps, onto a wooden deck that was suspended over the water and into a large bedroom filled with natural light. 'This is your room. Have a rest, you deserve it. When you're ready for a massage or whatever takes your fancy, just pick up the phone and dial zero.'

Faith blinked. Her head was full of questions but she had no chance to ask any of them because he'd left the room.

It was like being dropped into paradise.

She slept in the enormous, comfortable bed and then lay in the shade on the deck while a girl rubbed scented oils into her skin, the skilful stroke of her fingers removing all the last strands of tension from Faith's body.

After the massage, she sat and gazed across the tranquil water of the lake while someone tended to her nails and another did her hair.

There was no sign of Raul and when she eventually walked back into her room, she wondered how she was supposed to contact him.

A splash of colour drew her eye and she glanced towards the bed, her eyes widening as she saw the beautiful silk dress laid carefully on the cover. The exquisite fabric shimmered in the late-evening light and Faith stepped towards it, puzzled. *Had Raul left this for her?* And then she saw the diamond necklace, draped almost casually across the bodice, the stones sparkling and glittering like shards of ice.

She was so stunned that it took her a few moments to notice the card. Her fingers shaking, she opened the envelope and read the dark, bold scrawl: *Every woman deserves to be given a silk dress and diamonds at least once in her life. Enjoy. R.*

Completely out of her depth, Faith stared at the dress and the necklace. It was an enormously generous gift. *Obviously* she couldn't possibly accept it.

She stood for a moment, her lip caught between her teeth, her eyes on the dress. Tormented by indecision, she stepped away from the bed and then immediately stepped back again. Then she let the dressing gown slip from her shoulders, the feminine side of her completely unable to let her ignore such a gorgeous dress.

She was just going to try it on. Nothing more than that.

Just for a minute.

The silk slithered over her skin and she gave a moan of indulgence as she realised that it was a perfect fit.

How had he guessed her size?

Feeling as though she was living someone else's life, Faith fastened the dress and then tried to secure the clasp of the necklace. Strong fingers covered hers and swiftly finished the job.

Stifled by sexual awareness, she turned

slowly and found herself looking into Raul's laughing eyes.

'So how is your day going?' His fingers lingered at the base of her throat. 'Do you feel properly thanked?'

'I can't possibly accept any of this.'

'Of course you can. It is nothing.'

To him, maybe, but she suspected that the necklace alone was worth more than she earned in a year. 'I'm just trying it on, that's all. And then I'm taking it straight off.'

'Why would you want to do that?'

'Because this is *not* my life.'

He turned her gently until she was facing the mirror. 'So who is that, if it isn't you?'

Faith barely recognised herself. Her hair fell past her shoulders like sleek, polished gold, the diamonds glinted against her pale skin and the dress hugged her figure. She felt like a princess. 'Maybe I'll wear it just for this evening.' She almost laughed at her own weakness. 'But then I'm giving it back.'

Acknowledging her internal battle, Raul smiled. 'We'll have dinner on the terrace. The view is very pretty.'

* * *

'So do you do this often?'

He dismissed the staff with a discreet movement of his head and reached over to pour her another glass of wine. 'Eat dinner? Yes. All the time.'

'No, I mean—' She glanced down at herself. 'Play the part of the fairy godmother.'

'It's fun buying gifts for a woman who appreciates them.' He watched her across the table. 'You're not eating. Aren't you hungry?'

Her stomach was churning so badly that she just couldn't touch the food. 'No. No, I'm not. Sorry. It looks really delicious but—'

He gave a slow smile. 'You don't need to apologise for the fact that I'm putting you off your food. I take it as a compliment.'

'You're very sure of yourself.'

'And you're very nervous, and I can't understand why. Don't they have men in England?'

Not men like him. 'I've been too busy working to notice men,' she said lightly and his eyes narrowed.

'You are very dedicated to your work. Why did you choose to become a vet?'

'I always wanted to. My father was a vet and I grew up helping alongside him. Even when I was small, he'd involve me in some way and he always encouraged me.'

'He is proud of you, I'm sure.'

Faith hesitated. 'He and my mother died two years ago,' she said quietly. 'That's one of the reasons I came to Argentina. I missed them so much and I knew I needed to do something different. I thought combining travel with work might be the distraction I needed.'

'What about marriage and babies?' His tone was casual but when she looked at him his gaze was sharp and incisive as if the answer to that question mattered to him. 'When women think about the future it almost always contains a wedding ring.'

'That's a typically Argentine-male comment,' she teased, giving up on her food and putting her fork down. 'Be honest—you don't think a woman can do anything except stay at home and breed, do you?'

'It's what most women want. Don't you?'

'No. Not right now. In the future? Who knows?' She glanced towards the stillness of the lake. 'The future feels miles away when you're out here. I'm too young to even think about that. I have my whole career ahead of me. In another ten years or so, maybe.' She shrugged. 'It just isn't what I want. I love my job.' She watched the sunset, admiring the shimmering red glow that was reflected in the still water of the lake. 'What about you? No wife? No babies?'

Something flickered in his dark gaze. 'Absolutely not.'

'You mean, you don't want it now.'

His long strong fingers tightened ruthlessly round the wine glass. 'I don't want it ever. Remember that, Faith.' There was a steeliness in his voice that made her look at him more closely but his handsome face revealed nothing.

She frowned, sensing undertones that she didn't understand and feeling puzzled by them. 'Why would I need to remember it?'

'It's just something that I like to make clear,' he said softly, 'early in a relationship.'

Heat rushed through her body. 'Are we having a relationship?'

'I don't know,' he replied softly, his dark eyes fixed on hers. 'Are we?'

CHAPTER THREE

Ten months later

'SHE just stepped in front of the taxi without looking. According to a man who witnessed the accident, she's lucky to be alive.'

Lucky?

Lying in the hospital bed, listening to those words, Faith decided that it was better to keep her eyes closed. *She didn't feel lucky.*

'Any news on next of kin?' The doctor spoke again and Faith felt the dull pain inside her intensify to serious agony.

No next of kin.

She'd lost *everything* and it was hard to know whether her injuries were more severe on the outside or the inside.

'None. She had no identification on her when she was brought in—they assume someone must have stolen her bag. Her dress was expensive, though,' the nurse murmured enviously. 'Some flashy designer label I couldn't afford in a month of Sundays. Take it from me, she's either got a good job or a very rich and generous boyfriend.'

'Well, we can't discharge her until we know she has a home to go to. It's very inconvenient because she's blocking a bed.' The doctor sounded impatient. 'Someone should have missed her by now.'

Only if someone cared, Faith thought bleakly. In her case, no one did.

'Faith? Are you awake?'

Resigning herself to the fact that they wouldn't go away until she'd spoken, Faith reluctantly opened her eyes and the doctor gave a wintry smile.

'How are we today?' He spoke in the faintly patronising tone that he obviously reserved for patients.

'I'm fine.' *No point in telling the truth.* 'Much better.'

'I expect you're longing to go home.'

Home? Where was home? For the past year it had been Argentina and she'd thought...

Faith turned her head away, realising with a sickening lurch of horror that she was going to cry. The misery had been bubbling up inside her for days and suddenly it felt almost too enormous to hold back.

With a huge effort of will, she tried to focus her mind on something neutral. She wasn't going to think about Argentina, she wasn't going to think about the fact that she didn't have a job or a home any more, but most of all she wasn't going to think about…

She gave a tortured groan and curled into a foetal position, her thoughts so agonising that she just wanted to remove them from her head.

'Are you in pain?' The doctor leaned towards her, frowning. 'I can give you something for it.'

Not for this type of pain. Faith squeezed her eyes tightly shut. 'It's all a hideous mess.'

'Your head? It's nothing that time won't heal. Your hair will cover the scar.'

'Not my head,' Faith muttered. 'My life.'

'She's obviously worrying about her head— how's the wound, nurse? Everything healing?'

Realising that no one was remotely interested in how she really felt, Faith kept her eyes closed, wishing they'd go away and leave her alone.

'Last time I saw it everything was healing beautifully,' the nurse said briskly. 'It will be a very neat scar.'

On the outside, maybe, Faith thought to herself. But on the inside it was a deep, ugly gash that would never heal.

Clearly oblivious to the true extent of his patient's trauma, the doctor gave a nod of approval. 'You've made a remarkable recovery considering the condition you were in two weeks ago. We need to start talking about discharging you.' He cleared his throat and glanced at the chart again. 'You need to go home to family or friends. You can't be on your own at the moment.'

Faith's lips were so dry she could hardly speak. 'I'll be fine on my own.'

Just saying the words intensified the sick throbbing in her head.

How had she ended up at this point?

The doctor gave an impatient sigh. 'You haven't given us details of your next of kin. There must be *someone*. Or do you think it's possible that you are suffering some degree of memory loss after all?'

Faith opened her eyes. 'My parents died nearly three years ago and I'm an only child,' she said wearily, wondering how many times she had to repeat herself. 'And my memory is fine.' *Unfortunately.* Given the nature of her memories, she would have paid a great deal for a serious bout of amnesia. Nothing too dramatic. As long as she lost all knowledge of the last couple of months, she'd be happy.

She wanted the whole nightmare erased from her head for ever.

But in her case it wasn't forgetting that was the problem, it was remembering.

She remembered *everything* and the memories tortured her.

All she wanted to do was cover herself with the duvet and just sob and sob and the fact that she felt like that was terrifying because it was so unlike her.

Where was her energy and drive? What had happened to her natural inclination to fight problems with grit and determination?

She'd always been resilient. Life could be tough, she knew that.

But although she'd always known that life could be tough, she'd had no idea it could be quite *this* tough.

Panicked by how truly awful she felt, she rolled onto her back and stared up at the cracked ceiling—but somehow the cracks looked like the curve of a beach and soon the images in her head were of a laughing, naked woman and a spectacularly handsome man.

She gave a groan of denial and covered her face with her hands. It didn't matter what she did or where she looked, the memories were everywhere. She felt drained and empty, lacking the physical or emotional energy to drag herself out of the dark pit of despair that was sucking her down and down.

In the bed opposite, an old lady rambled and muttered, confused and disorientated by her surroundings. 'Doctor, doctor!'

Muttering something under his breath to the nurse, the doctor turned. 'Yes, Mrs Hitchin?' His manner and tone were a study of exaggerated politeness. 'What can I do for you?'

'You can marry me, that's what you can do!' The old lady's tone was sharp. 'No more messing me around! Do what you promised to do and stop running away from your responsibilities.'

The nurse covered her mouth with her hand to conceal the laugh and the doctor's face turned a deep shade of beetroot.

'You're in *hospital*, Mrs Hitchin!' He raised his voice and separated each syllable, as if he were speaking to a very slow child. 'And I'm a doctor!'

'Well, I'm glad you finally made something of yourself.' The old lady waggled a finger at Faith. 'Don't believe a word he says to you. Men are all the same. They want all the fun and none of the responsibility.'

Faith gave a choked laugh. 'I could have done with that advice a few months ago, Mrs Hitchin.' Then perhaps she wouldn't have made such a complete and utter wreck of her life.

Another nurse hurried into the room, her cheeks flushed and her eyes glowing. Excitement radiated from her like a forcefield and she had the look of a woman just bursting with serious gossip.

Her eyes slid to Faith and her expression changed to one of awe and fascination. 'I know you think your memory is fine, Faith,' she said sympathetically. 'But I'm afraid we now have evidence that you are suffering from amnesia.'

Faith gritted her teeth. 'My memory is fine.'

'Really? Then why can't you remember that you're married? You're married to a billionaire,' the nurse said faintly. 'And he's standing outside right now waiting to claim you. I mean, he's gorgeous, sexy—'

'Nurse!' Dr Arnold interrupted her with a scowl and the nurse blushed.

'All I'm trying to say,' she muttered, 'is that he just isn't the sort of man any woman would ever forget. If she really doesn't remember him, then she *definitely* has amnesia.'

Simmering with impatience, Raul glanced at the Rolex on his wrist, oblivious to the fact that the force of his presence had brought the entire hospital ward to a standstill. Like a thoroughbred racehorse at the starting gate, he radiated coiled, suppressed energy, as confident and unselfconscious in this environment as he was in every other, his powerful legs planted firmly apart, his intelligent dark eyes fixed on the room straight ahead of him.

Female members of staff suddenly found reasons to hover around the central nurses' station, distracted by the unexpected presence of such a striking man.

Raul didn't notice.

He was entirely focused on the task in hand and this brief, unexpected delay in reaching his final objective was a thorn of irritation under his richly bronzed skin.

A lesser man might have spent the time worrying that the information he'd received might be wrong, *that it wasn't her*. Raul had no such concerns. He only employed the best. His security team had been hand-picked and the possibility that they might have made a mistake didn't enter his head.

Barely containing his impatience, he stood still for a full thirty seconds—which was twenty-five seconds longer than he'd ever waited for anything in his life before—and then took matters into his own hands and strode purposefully across the corridor and into the six-bedded side ward.

The doctor greeted his sudden entrance with a murmur of disapproval that Raul ignored. His gaze swept the room and came to rest on the slender figure of the woman lying in the bed by the window.

The anger that had been building inside him erupted with lethal force and he ran his hand over the back of his neck in order to stop himself from punching something. And then he took a closer look at the solitary figure staring up at the ceiling and the anger died, only to be replaced by a surge of very different emotions.

Emotions that he didn't want to feel. Primitive urges that mocked his belief in his own sense of discipline and self-control.

Raul almost laughed. The weakness of man was woman, and that hadn't changed since the beginning of time. From Eve in the Garden of Eden and Pandora with her box, for every man there was one woman who seemed to be designed for the express purpose of complicating life.

And for him, that woman was lying in front of him.

He could negotiate the most complex business deal without once losing his clarity of thinking but here, in the same room as her, a witch's cauldron of emotions stirred to life, clouding everything.

'Faith.' His strong voice reverberated round the small room and her head turned, her expressive green eyes widening with horror and disbelief as she saw him.

'No!' Immediately she shrank under the blankets and her reaction was like a fist in his gut but the biggest shock was seeing the remains of the bruises on her face and shoulders before they vanished under the covers.

'What happened to you?' Two weeks before her mouth had been permanently curved into a happy smile and her blonde hair had rippled down her back. Now it was cropped short in a rough, jagged style that made her eyes look huge and her face pale and vulnerable. And there was no trace of the cheeky, teasing smile that was so much a part of her.

Kiss me, Raul, go on. You know you want to. Forget about work.

That one brief glance had been enough to show him that she'd lost weight. She'd always been fine-boned and delicate but now her skin seemed almost preternaturally pale and her jagged haircut gave her face an almost ethereal quality. When had that happened?

Why hadn't he noticed?

Something tugged at him and he ruthlessly pushed the feeling away.

She'd brought this on herself. And on him.

The doctor cleared his throat. 'We were forced to cut her hair when we were dealing with her injuries.'

'*Dios mío*, she's skin and bone.' Caught broadside by emotions that he hadn't expected, Raul directed the full force of his anger towards the doctor. 'Don't you *feed* your patients in this hospital?'

Clearly unaccustomed to such full-on confrontation, the doctor fiddled nervously with the charts he was clutching. 'Faith suffered a head injury,' he stuttered. 'She was unconscious for a while. Her rapid recovery is nothing short of remarkable. We saved her life.'

'Good,' Raul said coldly, his eyes focusing on the doctor's badge as he committed the name to memory. 'Because if you hadn't then your days of practising medicine would now be over. How was she injured?'

The nurse stepped forward swiftly, obviously hoping to smooth the situation. 'According to witnesses, she walked in front of a car just outside the airport terminal. It was as if she wasn't looking.'

Raul strode over to the bed, his mouth tightening as she turned her back on him and pulled the covers even higher.

That simple gesture said more than words ever could and suddenly he was gripped by the unfamiliar tentacles of guilt. He thrust them aside, reminding himself that he had no reason to feel guilty.

She'd done this to them.

He'd been up front and honest from the start. *She* was the one who'd chosen to play elaborate female games. And it was time she acknowledged that. 'Look at me!'

The lump in the bed didn't move and he gave an exasperated sigh. 'Running from a problem solves nothing. *Have you any idea how worried I've been?'*

The anger had burned inside him day and night for the past two weeks and he'd promised himself that when he finally caught up with her he would make sure that she was left in no doubt about his feelings.

For a moment he thought she wasn't going to respond and then the figure in the bed moved slowly and she sat up.

The words died in his throat.

There was something about her appalling fragility that prevented him from venting the full force of his wrath. She looked as vulnerable and shaky as one of his newborn foals and Raul felt something twist inside him.

He'd always thought of her as strong and vibrant, but there was no sign of the energy and enthusiasm that he'd come to expect from her.

The shapeless hospital nightdress hung from her narrow shoulders, her eyes were shaded by dark bruises and there were scratches on her shoulders and arms.

The usually irrepressible sparkle in her green eyes had been extinguished and she stared straight forward, refusing to meet his gaze.

She looked like a woman who was broken.

Apart from that one, anguished word—
'No!'—she hadn't spoken or glanced in his direction since he'd entered the room. It was as if
she was pretending that he wasn't there.

Reflecting on the damage she'd caused, Raul felt
another monumental surge in his tension levels.

Was she sorry? *Did she regret what she'd done
to their relationship?*

He stared in brooding silence at her frozen
profile. If it had been any other woman he would
have walked away and left her to deal with the
situation she'd created. But Faith wasn't any
other woman and something kept his feet nailed
firmly to the ground.

Pandora, Eve, *Faith…*

Exasperated with his own display of
weakness, Raul turned back to the doctor who
was now eyeing him with trepidation. 'What
are her injuries?'

'Well—er—' The doctor cleared his throat.
'Despite the seriousness of the accident, she has
made a remarkable recovery. She experiences
some headaches and a little dizziness from time
to time, but the wound on her head is healing
well. There is, however, the issue of her

memory.' Accustomed to relatives who were suitably submissive and respectful, he was obviously struggling to cope with Raul's direct, forceful approach. 'We have found it difficult to assess the extent of her amnesia.'

'She doesn't have amnesia.' It had taken only one glance for Raul to know that she remembered absolutely everything that had happened between them.

The doctor looked taken aback. 'But—she doesn't appear to remember you.'

Raul's mouth tightened into a grim line and he transferred his gaze to the frozen profile of the woman on the bed. 'Oh, she remembers,' he said softly. 'If her memory was impaired, she wouldn't be ignoring me. She'd be firing sparks and demanding to know why I took so long to get here. The reason she is refusing to look me in the eye is because her memory is perfectly intact and she's suffering from a severe attack of guilty conscience, isn't that right, *cariño*?'

Her head turned at that, her gaze locked with his and although she didn't say a single word her eyes sent him straight to hell.

The past swirled and bubbled between them

like a dangerous beast just waiting to swallow them whole.

Then she looked at the medical staff. 'I don't know who he is,' she said, her voice remarkably steady. 'I've never seen him before in my life and I don't like the look of him. It would be quite wrong of you to release me into his care.'

Raul gave a bitter laugh. Ignoring the notices about not sitting on the bed, he settled his powerful frame only inches away from her body. 'They have no choice but to release you into my care. I'm your only family.' He thought her eyes grew brighter but when he looked more closely she was staring straight ahead, still studiously ignoring him.

The doctor cleared his throat. 'You have to admit that her memory seems cloudy where you're concerned—'

'I've discovered that Faith's memory is most adaptable,' Raul drawled. 'Occasionally she can forget the most important facts. Like an agreement between two people.' His words had the desired effect and he watched with grim satisfaction as the last of the colour drained from her cheeks.

'There was no agreement. I am *not* one of your business deals. I wish I'd never met you. I *hate* you, Raul. You are a heartless, cynical, insensitive…' Her voice tailed off and the doctor gave a small, embarrassed cough.

'Well—it does appear that she at least knows your name so that's good. And—er—a little bit about your personality. She told us that she had no family—'

'I don't have family.'

The doctor glanced at her and then at Raul. 'I suppose—' He coughed nervously. 'Well, over to you, really.'

'That's it? Are you just going to stand there and let him bully you?' Faith glared at the doctor and when the man didn't reply she made a sound of disgust. 'You're all spineless. I'm telling you, he's *not* my family. If I was the last woman left on the planet and he was the last man, then the human race would die.' Having drawn the battle lines, she turned her head back to Raul and her eyes locked with his in fierce combat.

Raul felt a surge of relief because for a moment he'd wondered if her lack of spirit was something to do with the head injury. But the dangerous shimmer in her eyes reassured him that her accident hadn't done any permanent damage and despite everything that had happened between them he felt the instantaneous response of his body.

Passion. Hot, searing, blinding passion.

It was always there between them, whatever they were doing.

And that was the problem of course. Their astonishing physical compatibility had made it all too easy to overlook the truth.

They were two people who should never have been together.

Both of them had known it, but the extraordinary chemistry had bound them together when common sense should have dragged them apart.

She was *entirely* wrong for him. *He* was *entirely* wrong for her.

Somehow that hadn't made a difference.

Aware that the medical staff were rooted to the spot, staring, he rose to his feet and took charge.

'She has family,' he said in a driven tone. '*I'm* her husband. And I'll take over from here.' Detaching himself from the emotional, he concentrated instead on the practical, his mind shifting into problem-solving mode as he reached into his pocket for his mobile phone.

'Oh, here we go,' Faith muttered. 'Let's just make another million while we're hanging around.'

Having accessed a number with a decisive stab of his finger, Raul turned with a mocking smile. 'I wouldn't bother switching the phone on for a million, *cariño*. You should know that by now.'

The doctor cast them both a despairing glance. 'The two of you clearly have some problems.'

Rising to his feet, Raul dealt the other man a glance that would have silenced a football stadium in full voice. 'Unless you're adding psychiatry to your list of questionable medical skills, I suggest you don't tread where you are bound to lose your footing. She is no longer your responsibility. I'll be removing her from this place in the next ten minutes.' Having delivered that missile directly to its target, Raul turned his attention to the man on the end of the phone and switched to his native Spanish.

By the time he'd ended the call, the nurse had retreated and the doctor was sifting through paperwork with shaking hands, clearly worrying about his own position.

'If you're taking her then you'll have to sign something. I won't be held responsible if anything happens to her. She *needs* to be in hospital—'

'Maybe. But not this one.' With one disdainful sweep of his eyes, Raul took in the state of the ward. 'What exactly *is* this place and why hasn't it been shut down before now?'

'Shut down?' The doctor looked scandalised. 'This is the oldest hospital in London. We have been treating patients in this building since the time of King Henry the Eighth!'

'It's a shame no one has bothered to clean the floors since his last visit,' Raul said coldly and the old lady in the bed opposite Faith clapped her hands in delight.

'Oh, well said! I do so love a man who is dominant *and* handsome. These days most men have forgotten how to be *real* men. If she turns you down, I'm available.'

Amused, Raul turned and flashed her a smile. '*Gracias*, I will remember that.' His response clearly goaded Faith because she gave a strangled laugh.

'He's the worst of a bad bunch. If you're looking for a man who shoulders responsibility, then don't look at this one, Mrs Hitchin.'

'I could look at him all day,' Mrs Hitchin said happily, adjusting her hearing aid. 'I think he's *gorgeous*.'

'Actually he's a sex-mad control freak,' Faith muttered and Raul gave a twisted smile.

'One wonders why, with that glowing opinion of my qualities, you were so grimly determined to drag me to the altar by any means at your disposal.'

Faith lifted her chin and her beautiful eyes flashed at him. 'I did *not* drag you. Since when have you ever done *anything* that didn't suit you? Your life is one long selfish, self-indulgent ego trip.'

'You put me in an *impossible* position!' His tone thickened, Raul felt his tension levels soar into the stratosphere. He hadn't intended to tackle the issue here but even without spelling it out it was there in the room with them, hovering between them.

He saw that she was shaking and his eyes scanned the pale flesh of her smooth, slender arms, his treacherous mind turning to thoughts of sex. Those arms had been entwined round his neck, curved round his body as she'd urged him on. Those eyes that now flashed in anger had softened and tempted as she'd lured him on an erotic journey from which neither of them had emerged unscathed.

What they had shared was so powerful that even now he could taste it in the air. Even now, with all that lay between them, he knew that he could turn her from spitting hell-cat to purring kitten with one skilful touch of his mouth.

Only with supreme effort of will did Raul prevent himself from reaching out and flattening her against the bed.

And she knew.

She'd always known the effect she had on him. And she'd loved to tease and prolong the agony for both of them, using those jewel-bright green eyes of hers to raise the temperature from hot to raging inferno. With sideways glances, slow smiles and the sensuous swing of her hips she'd stoked the fire of his libido, pushing and pushing until his control had finally cracked. And when it had, she'd taken him into her soft, pulsing body, her desperation matching his.

In some ways their entire relationship had been a power struggle.

And for a while she'd won.

Only she was showing no signs of celebrating her victory.

'Just get out, Raul,' she said, and her voice held a quiver of vulnerability that he hadn't expected. 'It's over. You wanted an escape, well, I'm giving you one. Get out.'

'It would have been a great deal better for both

of us had you realised that a few months ago. As it is, your timing is unfortunate. I'm your husband, *cariño*, although you could be forgiven for forgetting that fact, given that we were married for all of two hours before you ran away.'

'I didn't run away. I'm not a child or a convict. I left because I discovered what a *monumental* mistake I'd made about you. I wouldn't have married you at all if I'd known what you were like.'

Remembering the circumstances of their wedding, Raul gave a bitter laugh. 'I think we both know that isn't the case. Anyway, you made your bed and fortunately for you it's a great deal more comfortable than the one you're lying in at the moment.'

'I'm not going with you, Raul, and you can't make me. I'm not one of your staff.'

'If one of my staff had behaved the way you did,' he snapped, 'they would no longer be working for me. Unfortunately we are now legally bound, so firing you isn't an option. Believe me, I've considered it.' His phone rang and he took the call, simmering with dark, deadly emotion, his eyes on hers as he listened and then broke the connection.

'My plane has been refuelled, a medical team

is now on board and we take off in an hour from now.'

She shrank away from him. 'I'm not well enough to go with you. I haven't fully recovered.'

'Then you can complete your recovery in the sunshine by my pool,' he returned in a cool tone and she flopped back against the pillows, looking drained and exhausted. Raul wondered grimly whether her pallor was a reflection of the effort the confrontation had required, or the fact that she was contemplating the reality of being back in a marriage that she never should have entered in the first place.

You wanted a war, my beauty, he thought bitterly, and you fired the first shot. *Now live with the consequences.*

CHAPTER FOUR

TWENTY-FOUR hours later, Faith was lying on a sun-lounger under the shade of a huge umbrella. In front of her lay the perfectly still waters of the most stunning pool she'd ever seen and all around her a profusion of exotic plants and trees gave her the impression of being deep in a lush rainforest.

Once they'd landed in Buenos Aires she'd expected him to take her straight back to the *estancia*, but instead he'd taken one look at her pale face and given instructions for them to be taken straight to the Vásquez building, his corporate headquarters in the smartest district of the vibrant South American city.

She'd swiftly discovered that his corporate headquarters was crowned by a breathtaking penthouse apartment, complete with a lush, exotic roof garden.

He'd taken her straight up to this outdoor paradise but she found herself wondering about the apartment. When did he use it? And what for?

Already aware of just how little she knew him, this further question gnawed away inside her but she forced herself not to think about it. She had other, more pressing issues demanding her attention: like the reason he'd brought her back to Argentina.

When she'd stumbled away from him on their wedding day, she hadn't thought for a moment that he'd follow her. Why would he, when he'd made it perfectly clear that he didn't love her?

Remembering the things that he'd said to her, she gave a shiver.

She'd been so utterly shocked by what had happened that her only thought had been to get as far away from him as possible.

For the sake of her own mental health, she'd known that she could have nothing more to do with him. She'd felt dead inside, as if the most important part of her had been gouged out. She'd loved him *so* much and the ten months they'd spent together had been the happiest of her life.

It was almost impossible to believe that it had all gone so dramatically wrong.

That she'd been so wrong about him.

Faith reached for the glass of chilled lemonade that had been left within her reach and took a sip, completely unable to relax because she knew that Raul would reappear at some point.

What was he doing? Was he working? How could he work when their marriage was in its death throes?

She glanced up and saw him strolling across the sun-baked terrace towards her. He'd showered and changed after the flight and was now wearing a pale shirt with lightweight trousers. An air of leashed power emanated from his tall, athletic frame and Faith's mouth dried.

For a moment she had no idea what to say to him. She wanted to shout at him, she wanted to hit him until she made dents in that spectacular body of his, but most of all she just wanted to lie down and sob because it just never should have been like this between them.

In the end she just stayed on the sun-lounger and didn't move, too drained to do any of the things in her mind.

The fact that he looked perfectly groomed despite the pressure of the situation came as no surprise to her. Raul had been born and bred in

Buenos Aires and if there was one thing that her travels in South America had taught her, it was that the body-conscious Brazilians were nothing compared to the pride of the average Argentine male.

In fact, Raul was less obsessed than most but she'd long ago come to the conclusion that that was because he was so much more beautiful than most. He didn't have to try. Even if he never glanced in a mirror again, he would still be unable to walk down a street without attracting an almost stifling degree of dazed female attention.

'Next time you decide to run away, stop when you reach the end of the drive,' he advised in an acid tone. 'I have just spent the entire morning unravelling problems that occurred while I was chasing you across the globe.'

'I didn't ask you to come after me.'

'You left me no choice. If you wanted an open marriage, you shouldn't have picked a South American male.' He turned his head and miraculously a team of staff appeared.

Faith watched in silence as they laid a table and served lunch. 'I'm not hungry.'

'You need to eat.'

She glanced at him then and immediately

wished she hadn't because it was immediately apparent that the way he'd treated her hadn't done anything to reduce the physical impact of the man.

He was well over six feet tall, lean and hard muscled and he moved with a predatory grace that was unequivocally male. Strong and athletic, he pushed himself to the limits in every aspect of his life—work, play, exercise, *sex*—for Raul it was all about being the best and he accepted nothing less.

'Don't let me hold you up,' she said politely. 'I'm sure you're dying to eat and return to your work.'

'Having solved the immediate crisis I have no intention of working this afternoon.' His expression grim, he sat down on one of the chairs and served himself. 'There are more important issues at stake.'

'More important than your work?' Despite everything that lay between them, she found herself laughing but she stopped herself quickly because she couldn't be sure that it wasn't going to end in a sob. 'And I thought I was the one who had the bang on the head.'

She felt strangely disconnected, making polite conversation with a man who didn't know the meaning of the term, when beneath the surface of conventional chat there lay a deep chasm of trouble and turbulence.

They'd never resorted to 'polite' before.

Their entire relationship had been a full-on explosion of exquisite passion, so uncontrolled and ferocious in its intensity that it had burned everything in its path.

She'd been crazy about him. And crazy to get involved with him when she had known his reputation for hurting women.

What had made her think she would be different?

What had made her think she could handle him when plenty of women before her had tried and failed?

She'd thought she understood him but she'd discovered too late that she'd barely scratched the surface. Raul Vásquez was a complex, volatile man, his character so full of dark, hidden corners that she suspected no woman would ever know him.

And now she was seeing a different side to him—the side that had made him a billionaire.

He was sharply intelligent but instead of his usual dry observations and smart comments, he was focused and on his guard. *Intimidating.* She'd been brought up to question and challenge and never to be afraid of anyone, but there was something about the harsh lines of his impossibly handsome features that made her want to just shrink into silence.

Over the past couple of weeks she'd gone from lover to adversary and no one in their right mind would choose Raul as an opponent.

His sexy mouth was set in a grim line and the unshakeable confidence that had made her weak at the knees made him seem more formidable than ever.

No wonder everyone just rolled over and played ball when he walked into a room, Faith thought hopelessly as she watched him take a sip of wine. In his current mood he wasn't a man that anybody would bother challenging.

Faith felt her stomach drop and told herself it was just part of the head injury. Hadn't they warned her she'd feel nauseous from time to time? It was nothing to do with Raul's presence. She couldn't possibly still feel anything for him. Not after what he'd said to her. What he'd *believed* of her.

Their relationship was dead in the water.

And she really didn't know what he was doing here.

He rolled his shoulders to ease the tension and despite all her determined resolutions, Faith's eyes were drawn to the swell of muscle visible beneath the fabric of his shirt. He had an incredible body. Hard, strong, powerful and capable of encouraging an unbelievable response from hers.

Raul caught the look and his eyes darkened. *'Don't,'* he warned and his eyes seemed to deepen in colour to a dangerous, stormy shade of black. *'Don't* look at me like that and *don't* bring sex into this or so help me I'll—' He broke off, his emotions so close to the surface that he clearly didn't trust himself to finish the sentence.

'Do you seriously think I'm lying here thinking about sex?' Her defence was attack, but the truth was that she *had* been thinking about sex and she knew that while she was still able to breathe, this man would always have that effect on her. *And she on him.* There was something between them that transcended all the rules.

One look was all it took.

One look was all it had ever taken.

And that was why they were here, of course, in this horrible mess.

If the physical attraction hadn't been so overwhelming, perhaps they would have discovered their fundamental differences a great deal sooner.

Abandoning the food on his plate, he made an

impatient sound and dropped the fork with a clatter. 'I don't know what you're thinking and I've given up guessing,' he growled. '*Why* did you run?'

She gasped and suddenly her palms literally ached with the desire to swipe the arrogant look from his indecently handsome face. 'If that is a serious question then you're even more insensitive than I think you are.'

'I am not insensitive.' He pushed the chair back and it scraped on the terrace, the dark flash in his eyes hinting at the degree of volatility that lurked beneath the veneer of control and sophistication. 'But I fail to see why anyone would go to the lengths you went to and then just walk away.'

'The lengths I went to?' Her voice shook. 'You make me sound like some sort of manipulative gold-digger.'

He looked at her and the derisive glint in his eyes spoke volumes. 'Yes?'

She swallowed, determined not to cry in front of him. How could he think that of her? 'I walked away because the things you said to me were *awful*! Heartless, callous and cruel. Did you really think I'd stick around for second helpings? I was hurt and sad—I needed support—and all I got was a double helping of blind, cynical insensitivity.'

His gaze locked on hers with the deadly accuracy of a heat-seeking missile. 'You created the situation. You should have stayed to see it through.'

'What was the point of that?' she forced herself to answer. 'You made your position more than clear. Hearing it once was bad enough.' *Enough to kill her dreams and her childish, naïve belief that they'd had something special.*

'If you are going to run at the first sign of trouble, our marriage is going to be extremely interesting.' He was infuriatingly sure of himself, forceful and arrogant, if he thought he could make her bow to his will by simply applying sufficient psychological pressure. 'If you'd talked to me, we could have sorted it out.'

'You weren't "talking" Raul. You were accusing! Judge and jury rolled into one—only you weren't prepared to listen to my defence.' She broke off in horror, unable to believe what she'd just said. 'You see what being with you has done for me? You've turned me from a rational, questioning human being into a meek, subservient blob with no brain! I don't need a defence because I've done *nothing wrong*!'

'You are the least subservient woman I have

ever met,' he said through gritted teeth. 'And I have never questioned your intelligence.'

'Then why are you behaving like this, Raul? Why are you so willing to believe the worst of me? You're talking as if I committed a crime, but you were there too!'

'You assured me that you were protected.'

'I thought I was!'

There. It was out. The subject that both of them had been avoiding since he'd first strode into her hospital ward.

She was trembling now despite the blazing sunshine, tiny shivers that took over her whole body, but whether it was as a reaction to her accident or his words, she didn't know. 'I didn't mean to get pregnant.' And she wasn't prepared to have this conversation. *Hadn't thought that he'd follow her.* 'Go away,' she croaked. 'Go back to your work because that's all you really care about. We no longer have anything else to say to each other.'

Her response sent shards of hostility cracking through the air and Raul rose to his feet and walked away from her, as if he were considering precisely that option. But he didn't leave the terrace. Instead he stood still, all coiled, suppressed tension like a jungle cat ready to leap on the first unwary animal that crossed its path.

She knew him well enough to know that he was at the outer limits of his patience and that surprised her because it was his razor-sharp thinking and icy control in all situations that had driven him to billionaire status. Where his competitors just cracked and folded under pressure, Raul showed nerves of steel.

But she still didn't understand why he had brought her here.

Searching for clues, she studied his taut, handsome profile through a hot haze of tears, noticing with almost detached curiosity that the hard lines of his jaw were darkened by stubble. Since when had Raul ever forgotten to shave?

Somehow that observation made her feel better.

If she was suffering then she wanted to know that he was suffering, too.

He turned back to her, control firmly back in his grasp, his tone icily formal. 'How are you feeling, physically? Have the medical staff I employed treated you well?' Deliberately he'd stepped aside from the unstable, shifting surface of their emotions.

'They've been fine.' She was equally polite.

'Offhand I can't think of a single person you need to fire or sue.'

A ghost of a smile touched his firm mouth as he acknowledged her accurate assessment of his personality. 'I think that comment confirms that your brain is still in perfect working order.'

'My brain is fine. *I'm* fine. You can let them all go now. They must be costing you a fortune.'

'"They" are one of the perks of being my wife, *cariño*.'

'I was never interested in your money and you know it.' The first time they'd met she hadn't even known about his money. It was only after she'd been scorched alive by the chemistry between them that she'd discovered his real identity. And by then it hadn't mattered. Nothing had mattered, not even the fact that he was difficult and complex. She'd thought she had what it took to handle him.

She'd been wrong.

She lifted her chin. 'When I met you, I had a career. Don't insult our relationship by implying that your money was ever part of what we shared.'

'So why are you worrying about cost? We have enough problems piled up between us. Let's not add more.' His tone harsh, he swept aside her protest with a single, decisive stroke and she sank against the sun-lounger, all the energy draining out of her.

'I'm worrying because we're not together any more and I don't want to owe you anything.'

'Now I'm starting to wonder whether your brain might be damaged after all.' He stood looking at her, his legs planted firmly apart in a stance that shrieked control. 'Did you walk under that car on purpose?'

She gasped with shock. *'No!* How can you ask me that?'

'Because I don't shirk from the difficult or the awkward,' he ground out. 'Unlike you. You were upset.' His hard stare allowed her no escape and Faith felt a sudden stab of agony.

Upset?

It was such an insignificant word to describe the utter devastation inside her. 'Of course I was upset. And that's why I didn't look where I was going.' She'd been blind with misery, her brain disconnected from everything except the enormity of her loss.

'You told the hospital that you had no next of kin. I can't believe that you were capable of such unbelievably selfish behaviour. *Why didn't you call me?'* His tone was thickened by raw, red, molten anger and this time when she looked at him her eyes were dry.

'Why would I have called you?'

His features were set and grim. 'It should have been obvious to you to let me know that you were safe.'

'I had no reason to believe you'd even care.'

'Now you're being childish.'

'I'm being honest! Our last meeting was hardly a loving encounter—you hurt me, Raul. *You hurt me so much.'*

'I was honest about my feelings.' His savage rejoinder showed no hint of self-reproach or apology and her shivering intensified, as if someone had dropped her in the Arctic wearing nothing more than her underwear.

'You don't have feelings and I can't do this, Raul. I don't know you any more. You're not the man I was with.' Her head was spinning alarmingly and her stomach rolled and lurched. 'Go away. Just go away. It's over, Raul.'

He swore softly and fluently and turned away from her, as if he didn't trust himself to look at her and not explode. 'Perhaps you didn't *want* to know me. This is who I am, Faith. The real me.

You saw only what you wanted to see. What suited you.'

'That isn't true. I know you can be ruthless in business, but you're *not* cruel, I know you're not.' The threat of tears was back with a vengeance and she blinked rapidly to clear her vision. 'Up until our wedding day you were—'

'What?' He turned, his dark eyes glinting hard. 'I was *what*? A complete fool? A trusting idiot?'

'I don't think it's foolish to trust the person you—' She just stopped herself saying the word 'love' because she knew now that he'd never loved her. 'Marry,' she said flatly. 'It's not foolish to trust the person you marry.'

'Oh really?' His tone was heavy with sarcasm. 'Perhaps that depends on the reason for the marriage. In our case it was based on deceit. Hardly a firm foundation for trust.'

'I did *not* deceive you! And I don't even understand why you would think that. Is this because of your money? Is this some sort of billionaire thing? What, Raul? You have so much money and you're such a fabulous catch that women are going to go to any lengths to trap you? Is that what this is about?'

Raul ran a hand over his face. 'We will leave

this subject aside for now.' His voice shook with emotion. 'You're not up to discussing it and frankly I'm not sure I am either.' It was a measure of his focus and determination that he was capable of moving on from a subject that was burning both of them up inside. 'You could have been killed.'

'And that would have solved your problem, Raul.'

'*Dios mío*, that comment is *totally* unjustified.' His tone was savage and loaded with contempt. 'Never at any point in this whole miserable mess have I wished you dead.'

Her head throbbed and her mouth was dry as a desert. Seeking any excuse to look away from him, Faith reached for the lemonade again but her hand was shaking so much that half of it slopped over her dress.

Raul stood still, exasperation flickering across his handsome face as he watched her efforts. Then he gave a soft curse and took the glass from her hand, his mouth compressed into a thin line as he held the glass to her lips. 'Drink.' His sharp command made her flinch but although there was no sympathy in his tone, he held the glass carefully, allowing her to take small sips before placing the glass back on the table.

But his attentiveness, albeit reluctantly given, simply made things worse.

He was so close to her and she breathed in his clean, male scent and felt her insides stir. It was as if her body recognised him and despite the heat, her shivering intensified.

Why couldn't he be less of a man?

Maybe then her brain and body would have worked in harmony instead of battling like opposing forces.

'Stop shivering.' Raul delivered the order in a driven tone but when his demand had no effect he reached for his phone. 'I will get the doctor back up here.'

'No.' Her teeth chattering, Faith shrank away from him, exhausted and wishing that he was easier to understand. He'd made it obvious that he bitterly regretted their wedding and yet he'd sought her out and brought her back to Argentina. 'Why did you bring me back here, Raul? Why?'

'You're my wife. You belong by my side and in my bed.'

That simple statement encompassed everything it meant to be married to an Argentine male and she closed her eyes briefly. So it was all about possession. There was no love there at all.

'I didn't want this to happen to us—'

'Yes, you did.' His words and his tone were brutal, leaving her no escape. 'You made this decision. You rolled the dice and you gambled. At least have the courage to face what you did to our relationship.'

The sick throbbing in her head intensified. 'I don't want to talk about it.'

He gave a bitter laugh. 'And that from a woman? Talking is what women are supposed to do best, isn't it, Faith? You think that every problem can be solved if it's talked through.'

Not every problem.

'I have nothing more to say to you, Raul. You're angry and bitter and I just don't know you any more.'

Something flickered across his dark, handsome face—dangerous shadows, a suggestion of something ugly lurking deep, deep inside.

'I can't be married to a man who doesn't love me,' Faith whispered. 'I want a divorce. Give me whatever you need me to sign and I'll sign it.'

Her flat statement drew no response from him and in the end she looked back at him, only to find that he'd walked towards the pool and was standing with his back to her.

Faith stared at him helplessly. Even from the back he was spectacular. His shoulders were wide and powerful, his legs strong and well-muscled. He carried himself with confidence, the astonishing success he'd made of his life evident in every aspect of his demeanour and behaviour.

Once, she'd believed he was hers.

She'd truly believed that they shared something special and the knowledge that for him their relationship had been empty hurt more than any of the wounds she'd incurred in the accident.

He turned suddenly, feeling her gaze on him with that instinctive awareness that had always bound them together. 'You went to all those elaborate lengths to get me to the altar and now you want a divorce?' His mouth twisted into a mocking smile. 'You're giving up extraordinarily easily. Take some advice—if something is worth fighting for, it's worth fighting to the death.'

It was a remark so typical of him that in the old days—*the days before marriage*—she would have smiled and teased him unmercifully. She would have told him to chill out and not be so driven. 'I never saw our relationship as a war, Raul.'

'You started the war. You manipulated me into marrying you,' he said coldly. 'So it seems absurd for you to abandon your goal so easily.' His supreme self-confidence and the chill in his tone simply added to her pain.

'I didn't have a goal, Raul!' Feeling at an even greater disadvantage lying down, Faith sat up. 'I'm not one of your companies!! I don't have a mission statement or a five-year plan! I did not manipulate you!'

'No? So who's fault is it that we are in this position? Marriage was *not* part of *my* plan. I was clear about that from the beginning.' He stepped forward, his voice throbbing with emotion. 'No marriage. No babies. You entered into our relationship with your eyes wide open.'

His words were so uncompromisingly harsh that for a moment she had trouble breathing.

They were *so* different. How could she ever have thought that their feelings for one another would be enough to bridge the gulf between them?

'It wasn't like that. We were just having fun, Raul. I wasn't even thinking about marriage.' Faith sank back against the sun-lounger. 'I thought we shared something special.'

'We did. But it wasn't enough for you, was it?

Like a typical woman, you wanted more and more.' His tone was an angry growl, his words so heavily loaded with accusation that she shrank. 'You thought that you knew what I wanted better than I did. Well, you were wrong *cariño*. I knew *exactly* what I wanted and it wasn't this.'

Every word he spoke was designed to destroy any last tender shoots of hope that might have survived the initial blast of his anger.

'You're still talking as if I had some sort of master plan. I didn't create this situation, Raul. I didn't lie to you.'

'You truly expect me to believe that it was an accident? Contraception is not a hit-and-miss affair.' He spelled it out with brutal lucidity and Faith felt her heart suddenly bump erratically.

He stood there like a mythical god—lean, arrogant and impossibly handsome, seeing everything from one point of view only.

His own.

'One day you'll learn that you can't control everything in life, Raul. Accidents *do* happen,' she said hoarsely. 'I am living proof of that, but it doesn't matter any more, does it?'

He drew breath, ready to challenge that remark

as he automatically challenged everything and she lifted a hand in a defensive gesture.

'No!' She cut him off before he spoke. 'Just don't say what's on your mind, Raul, because frankly I don't think I can sit through another session of your thoughts on the subject.'

'You don't know what I was going to say.'

'Oh yes I do. It would have been something along the lines of "if you hadn't got pregnant we wouldn't be married now" or "it's lucky for both of us that you lost the baby."' She'd been trying so hard not to think about the baby, but now there was no escaping it and her eyes filled with the tears that she'd been choking on for the past couple of weeks. 'Well, do you know what? I don't feel lucky. I know it wasn't what you wanted and to be honest, I was surprised myself—but I don't feel lucky, Raul. I *minded* that I lost the baby.'

He was so tense that every muscle in his powerful frame throbbed with it. 'I know.'

'*You do not know!* How could you know? I protected you from it. You were in New York on business. I was *devastated* but I kept it to myself because you were tied up with that meeting, takeover—'

'It was a merger.'

'*I don't care what it was!* I just knew it was important to you and I didn't want to cause you extra stress. But I shot myself in the foot, because you decided that the reason I didn't tell you about my miscarriage was because I was afraid you might call off the wedding.'

'It was a natural assumption.'

'Only for a man like you, Raul. Any other person would have thanked me for being so thoughtful and selfless.' She turned her head, her voice a whisper. 'Go away. Just go away. Why are we even talking about this, anyway?'

'Because we are married,' he bit out harshly. 'And we have to sort this out.'

'Some things just aren't fixable. And this is one of them. Do you realise that you haven't once thought about *my* feelings? All you've thought about is yourself. You think I trapped you. Well, do you know what?' Her voice rose. 'I wish you *had* ditched me at the altar. You would have been doing us both a favour.'

'I would not have done that. Despite what you think, I do have a sense of decency.'

'*Decency?* Where was your sense of decency when you said it was a good thing I'd lost the baby?'

He stiffened, his handsome face pale despite his tan. 'You are taking my words out of context.'

'I wish I was, but I'm not. And frankly, I would have preferred you to have broken it off, than to find myself married to a cold, insensitive bastard.'

He inhaled sharply. 'I've never heard you use language like that before.'

'Well, if you stick around, you'll be hearing more of it.'

Raul ran a hand over his face. 'You are *extremely* upset—'

'Yes. Funny that, really. I lose a baby, discover that my husband is a cold-hearted, ruthless pig, get run over—' Her heart was pounding so rapidly that she felt dizzy. 'I can't imagine why I'd be upset.'

'You need to calm down. The doctors said you shouldn't be subjected to any more stress.' Raul lifted a hand in what presumably was a gesture of conciliation. 'Why are we going over this again? *No me importa.* I don't care. It's history now. We have to move on.'

'Where to, Raul?' Faith choked, holding it together by a thread. 'You're relieved, but that isn't how I feel. I feel terrible. You have no idea. Our relationship is dead and so is—' She broke off with a whimper of pain, unable to finish the sentence. 'I wish there *had* been a baby.'

'I know you do.' Raul's tone was grim and his face was white with the strain. 'Which is why you should have left me six months ago for some homely, domesticated male whose sole desire was to reproduce and spread his seed. You should have ended it instead of forcing me into something I didn't want.'

'*It was an accident.*' She covered her face with her hands to hide the tears but clearly she was less than successful because she heard Raul swear and then felt his thigh brush against hers as he sat down next to her.

'*Stop* crying. I've never seen you cry before. You're the strongest woman I've ever met.' His strong fingers closed around her wrists and he pulled her hands away from her face, as if he could ease her distress simply by the force of his will. 'And you wonder why I am so against marriage as an institution! Until we exchanged vows, we were happy together.'

She sniffed. 'It isn't marriage. It's *you*—the way you are—'

'And you always knew the way I was. We both knew it, Faith.' Raul's tone was rough. 'There was never any future for us. Eventually you would have wanted marriage and babies. It was inevitable.'

'I hadn't even thought about it.' Furious with herself for crying, Faith wiped her eyes with the palm of her hand. 'I had a career when I met you. The last thing I was thinking of was playing happy families.'

'When you discovered how badly you wanted a baby, you should have left.'

'How are you so successful at negotiation when you don't even listen to the other person?' Faith bit back a hysterical laugh. 'That wasn't how it happened! I did not plan it. I had a whole career ahead of me. Plans! When I discovered that I was pregnant, I was in shock. But then I realised how much I wanted our baby.' And *him*. She'd realised how much she wanted him.

'And the fact that I didn't wasn't of importance to you?'

'You asked me to marry you!'

'Because you left me no choice.'

His blunt admission sliced through her control and brought the tears to the surface. 'Well, that's romantic. And having admitted that you married me because I "forced" you, you now want to continue this relationship? Are you mad, or what?' The tears trickled down her face and Raul's sensual mouth tightened.

'Don't cry.'

'Why?' The tears fell harder. 'Because it makes you feel bad? Well, good. At the moment, I *want* you to feel bad.' The utter desolation echoed in her voice and she saw his emotional turmoil.

After a moment's hesitation he reached out a hand towards her but she shrank away from him and he let it fall to his side. 'How did our relationship reach this point?'

'I don't know. I was so in love with you.' Her voice was thick with tears. 'I didn't think anything could ever damage what we had. I thought we were invincible.'

'And presumably that's why you did it.' His voice grew several degrees colder and she knew that she would never convince him that she hadn't become pregnant on purpose.

'So just divorce me,' she whispered, wiping her eyes with the back of her hand. 'Divorce me for unreasonable behaviour.'

'There won't be a divorce.' His tone was hard

and icy cold. 'You chose this path, *cariño*. Now walk it. I have some calls to make. Make sure you rest before dinner.'

CHAPTER FIVE

WHAT was she supposed to wear for dinner?

She'd fled from Argentina with nothing more than her passport. She certainly hadn't stopped to pack a wardrobe.

Glancing at her watch, she realised that there were still several hours until dinner, so she picked up her bag and stepped into the elevator.

They were in the centre of Buenos Aires. How hard could it be to find something simple and practical to wear?

She pressed the button for the ground floor, thinking of Raul. He'd changed *so* much and she didn't have to look far to discover the cause of their problems.

By becoming pregnant she'd committed the ultimate sin.

The lift doors opened and she gave a gasp of

shock because Raul was standing there, anger shimmering in his dark eyes.

'Do you have a death wish? You are supposed to be resting.'

For a long, agonising moment the tension throbbed between them momentarily blinding both of them. She was painfully aware of his sexuality and her stomach swooped and spun like a ride at a funfair.

Suddenly, looking at his rigid shoulders, she realised that they'd never stood a chance.

They were worlds apart; not just in terms of wealth, but in life experience and culture.

They'd talked all the time, but never about his past, and she was only now realising how little she knew about him.

The phone in his pocket rang and he removed it, scanned the number and then took the call. '*Sí*—I am aware of that.' He switched between Spanish and English with effortless ease and Faith listened with reluctant admiration, trying not to be impressed but failing because his razor-sharp intellect had always given her a buzz. She'd loved arguing with him because his brain was so fast and challenging him had always resulted in lively debate.

As if sensing her scrutiny, his eyes locked onto

hers and a muscle flickered in his jaw. 'No—cancel… I don't care, I'm busy right now. They can wait until I'm ready.'

Faith watched as he broke the connection with a decisive stab of one long finger and dropped the phone back into his pocket. She cleared her throat. 'If you were cancelling a meeting because of me then you shouldn't have bothered.'

'How else am I supposed to stop you from doing something foolish? If I don't watch you personally you will no doubt vanish again, and I have no desire to scrape you off the floor after yet another accident.' He'd obviously come from a meeting because he was dressed in a dark formal suit but the white cuff of his shirt had ridden up slightly and she found her eyes drawn to the hairs that darkened the bronzed skin at his wrist. That tantalising hint of masculinity was sufficient to trigger an uncomfortably vivid image of him naked and Faith turned her head away quickly, wondering how a physical connection could possibly endure when everything else was so catastrophically wrong between them. It was true that Raul exceeded the most exacting woman's standards of masculinity, but after everything that had happened, *she shouldn't be feeling this way.*

The brain was supposed to be connected to the senses, so why were hers humming and buzzing instead of freezing him off?

Glancing over his shoulder, Faith saw two burly men standing in the opulent lobby. 'Who are they?'

'Security.' Raul stepped into the elevator with her and slammed his hand against a button. He controlled his privacy with the same ruthless efficiency that he used on every other aspect of his life.

'I need to go shopping—'

'You were never interested in shopping.'

'I don't have anything to wear. All my clothes are at the *estancia.*'

He stared down at her for a moment. 'I apologise,' he said stiffly. 'I hadn't realised. You should have said something sooner.'

The doors slid closed and Faith suddenly found herself trapped with him in a small, intimate space.

Erotic images swirled around her brain and she stared straight ahead, trying to concentrate on something else. The utter stillness of his powerful body told her that he was doing the same thing and she knew instinctively that his brain was playing the same tricks.

So how could *not* looking intensify the connection between them?

In this closed-in space Faith was agonisingly aware of the latent power of his lean, strong body and she realised with a stab of pain that this was the first time she'd stood this close to him and not touched. In their relationship she'd been the affectionate one and he'd always teased her about it.

'You can't go five seconds without checking I'm still here.'

And it had been true. She'd adored him and it wouldn't have occurred to her to not show it.

But now she envied his emotional detachment and wished she'd kept part of herself back.

If she'd done that, would it hurt less?

Probably not. Despite everything that had happened between them, part of her wanted to take that final step towards him and feel his arms close around her in that decisive, possessive way that had always thrilled her.

And it *horrified* her that she still felt that way.

She couldn't be with a man who didn't trust her, could she? For her, trust was as fundamental as breathing. And she couldn't be with a man who had such little regard for her feelings. *A man who knew her so little.*

Did she have no self-respect?

Or was it just that she'd totally underestimated the power of love?

Desperate to interrupt the uncomfortable flow of her thoughts, Faith struggled to make conversation. 'I didn't know you had an apartment in Buenos Aires.'

He loosened his top button and jerked at his tie, the intimate confinement clearly affecting him in a similar manner. 'Sometimes I work late.'

The lift rose smoothly upwards and she stared at the view.

'It's stunning.'

'Actually it's on the market,' Raul said stiffly. 'I've discovered that a glass lift isn't a good choice if you want privacy.'

And Raul was fiercely protective of his privacy, she knew that. This particular billionaire wasn't about to become public property, and he invested time and effort into keeping his profile as low-key as possible. His extreme wealth had protected their relationship from the intrusion of the outside world.

She'd been spoiled, cosseted, protected and

most of the time she hadn't even been aware of that fact because everything in his life ran so smoothly and discreetly.

His main residence was the Beach House in the grounds of the *estancia*, ten thousand acres of prime real-estate that stretched from the Atlantic coast of Argentina into the grasslands. Under Raul's watchful eye, his dedicated staff, which had once included her, bred and trained polo ponies, and the *estancia* was the first port of call for the super-wealthy who enjoyed that particular sport.

With typical flare and vision, Raul had tapped into a market where the very, very rich would pay for the privilege of receiving the very best polo instruction and advice on the purchase of a string of ponies, safe from the prying eyes of the world's press. It also allowed Raul to indulge his dare-devil streak—as one of the country's most daring polo players, he thrived on the thrilling adrenalin rush of the game.

But the stud-farm was only a small part of an empire that encompassed hotels, finance and export. Applauded by the financial pages of the world's newspapers for his astonishing vision, Raul had diversified sufficiently to ensure that any change in the markets would have no effect on the overall profitability of his business.

The lift doors opened and Raul strode out, as if he couldn't wait to get away from her. After a moment's hesitation Faith followed, knowing that if she didn't do so voluntarily, he'd simply haul her out himself.

The penthouse apartment spread over the top of the building, a dazzling, soaring living-space designed to give the occupant breathtaking views over Buenos Aires.

'It is stunning,' she muttered weakly. 'Another world.' And at that moment she almost laughed at herself.

It *was* another world. The world he lived in. How had she ever thought she could just step into his life with no problems?

A frown touching his strong, dark brows, Raul turned his head and stared out of the window, as if the view wasn't something he'd noticed before. 'It's a city.'

His reply was so rigidly polite that Faith felt as though she was on a blind date with a stranger. 'If you didn't buy it for the view, why did you choose it?'

He gave a careless lift of his broad shoulders,

as if he considered it an odd question. 'I needed somewhere to shower and change in between meetings. And it's an investment.'

He was standing still but she could feel the energy pulsing from every centimetre of his powerful frame. She'd never met anyone as driven as Raul. 'Does money come into every decision you make?'

'Not always.' His charcoal-dark eyes locked on hers, his gaze boldly explicit and she understood the unspoken message in that one blistering look.

If he'd been thinking about money, he wouldn't have chosen her.

Looking at him now, at the careless arrogance he wore with the same ease as his expensive clothes, she wondered how she'd ever felt comfortable with him.

Everything about him screamed power and success but on top of that he possessed a raw, dominant sexuality that had always rendered her breathless.

For a moment his burning gaze held her captive, the sheer force of his personality preventing her from looking away.

In the end it was Raul who broke that connection, turning from her with a sudden movement that suggested an underlying tension of almost unbearable proportions. 'I haven't shown you round properly, but the bedroom is up the stairs.' His voice was tight, clipped, as if he were restraining himself not to say a great deal more. 'Take a shower and help yourself to some clothes from the wardrobe.'

Clothes? Her heart lurched and the dull, sick feeling in the pit of her stomach returned. Since when did he keep a spare set of clothes for female guests? She'd never been here, which could only mean that...

Reminding herself that the way he chose to live his life was no longer any of her business, Faith curled her fingers into her palms.

'Upstairs?'

'It's a duplex penthouse.' With a spare, minimal gesture he angled his glossy, dark head and she belatedly noticed a curving staircase in one corner of the room.

'Fine.' Not trusting herself to stay cool in front of him, she stalked across the apartment and up the stairs, horribly conscious of his eyes tracking her every movement.

She found herself in a sumptuous master-bedroom suite that extended over the whole of the top floor. Gripped by the sharp claws of jealousy, she kept her eyes firmly averted from the enormous bed. Raul had had women before her, she knew that. But she'd always told herself that they were part of his past.

Only now was it dawning on her that she'd never really known this dangerous, complicated, hotly sexual man. When he'd flown to Buenos Aires for meetings, had he been alone? Could Raul deprive himself of sex for a few nights? Remembering his almost insatiable hunger for her body, she doubted it. He was a man of apparently limitless stamina in every area of his life and the demands he placed upon himself would have exhausted a lesser man.

Reminding herself that none of that was supposed to matter to her any more, she made straight for the bathroom.

Even there she couldn't escape the vagaries of her imagination because the amazing glass bath was easily large enough for two, as was the shower.

And she knew enough of Raul's sexual appetites to know that he wouldn't have restricted his activities to the bedroom.

Trying to block out the distressing image of those skilled, bronzed hands on another woman, she stripped off her damp clothes and stepped under the shower. Why would she care that he had another woman? She didn't want him, did she? Not after what he'd believed of her. He was right—they were *totally* wrong for each other. She was a modern, thinking woman. He was a ruthless tycoon who inhabited a world she hadn't even known existed. And that world had made him cynical and hard.

She probably *should* have ended the relationship and maybe she would have if it hadn't been for the one small fact that he'd overlooked when he'd delivered that piece of advice.

She loved him.

Totally, completely and utterly. To the point where the mere idea of leaving would have been laughable.

And he'd taken that love and crushed it.

Closing her eyes, she let the hot water scald her skin, finding the warmth strangely soothing. After the clinical scent of the hospital it was pure bliss to lather indulgent products into her hair and body. She could have stayed under the shower for ever, but she knew that if she didn't emerge soon Raul would come looking for her and she didn't want that. Reluctantly she stemmed the flow of hot water, dried herself on one of the heated towels and walked into the dressing room.

Steeling herself for seeing a range of glamorous dresses, she was taken aback to see nothing but male clothing, both formal and casual.

Suits, shirts, ties, shoes—nothing remotely feminine or glittery.

Relief swamped her, closely followed by exasperation because she didn't want to feel anything. She didn't want to care. Shaking her head in despair, she wondered how she was ever going to divorce herself from this man. It wasn't the legal side that worried her—that would be simple enough. The real problem was the mental agony of accepting that he was no longer in her life.

Faith stared at the contents of his dressing room, realising with a sense of resignation that there was absolutely nothing that was going to fit her.

Abandoning ideas of boosting her flagging courage with a touch of power-dressing, she gave a shrug and reached for a crisp white shirt. She wasn't trying to make a good impression anyway, so what did it matter how she was dressed? The shirt fell to mid-thigh and she had to roll up the sleeves, but after she'd added a belt she decided that she was more or less respectable.

Feeling ridiculously self-conscious, she walked back into the luxurious living area.

Raul was standing with his back to her, phone to his ear as usual, his hand braced against the glass window as he listened to the person on the other end. For a moment Faith just watched him, her eyes feasting on every tiny detail from the fit of his shirt to the bold confidence that was so evident in everything he did. He was spectacular. Sleek, handsome and every inch the successful billionaire.

How had she ever thought that their relationship could work?

He was used to driving over everything in his path and she'd never been meek and submissive.

They'd been an accident waiting to happen.

Sensing her presence, he turned, issued a set of instructions and then terminated the call and dropped the phone onto the nearest available surface. His eyes swept over her in one swiftly assessing glance. 'You've lost weight.'

His comment shot like a spear through her self-confidence. 'Lost weight' good, or 'lost weight' bad? 'It's your shirt,' she muttered. 'It's too big for me. There weren't any female clothes.'

'Why would there be?' His tone was heavily

laced with sarcasm. 'On the whole I don't find the financial sector take me seriously if I arrive at a meeting wearing a dress.'

The question burned inside her and she looked at him, desperately wanting to ask and *hating* herself for that weakness. Their relationship was in its death throes. Why demean herself by voicing the fears that had been gnawing at her insides since he'd dragged her into the apartment?

The apartment she hadn't known about.

Raul shot her a look of sizzling impatience. 'You are *totally* transparent. But I don't play those games, Faith, I told you that when we first met. I was with you. I didn't want anyone else.'

The fact that he'd read her so easily should have bothered her but she was too lacerated by his use of the past tense to care. 'Women want you—'

'I'm an adult, not some hormonal teenager,' he said curtly. 'Do you think I jump into bed with every woman who looks at me?'

Obviously not, or he'd never get any work done.

Faith tried to breathe evenly. 'I just thought—'

'I know what you thought,' he snapped. 'And for your information I have never brought another woman here. This is convenient accommodation, not a love nest. When I'm here, I'm working.'

Wishing she hadn't exposed so much of herself, or her *feelings*, Faith looked away. 'This is so difficult.'

'You're the one who made it difficult.'

'You expect my trust but you don't give it in return.' She turned to him. 'What did I ever do to make you believe that I'd lie to you? And lie about something so enormously important?'

He stilled, his face ashen beneath his tan. 'You cannot walk around Buenos Aires wearing one of my shirts.'

So he was going to stampede right over the issue, then. Her legs gave way and she plopped onto the sofa. 'I didn't have any luggage.'

'You left Argentina with nothing?'

She wanted to turn the conversation back to the subject that he'd abandoned but her woman's intuition warned her that it was best left. If Raul was avoiding it, then he was avoiding it for a reason.

And suddenly she wanted to understand that reason.

Only now was it occurring to her that she was being punished for someone else's sins.

'When I left, I was upset, Raul.' In fact she'd been in such a state when she'd fled to the airport that it was fortunate her passport had been in her handbag or she wouldn't have gone far. 'I wasn't thinking.'

'Evidently.' The mockery in his voice was sharp as a blade. 'As you evidently weren't thinking when you stepped in the path of a taxi. You don't need luggage, *cariño*, you need protection. From yourself.'

'That's not true. And I wouldn't have taken any luggage, anyway.' She bit her lip. 'I didn't want to take anything that was yours.'

'*You* were mine,' Raul said with lethal emphasis, his thick dark lashes veiling the expression in his eyes. 'You were mine. And unlike you, I take incredibly good care of my possessions.'

CHAPTER SIX

'*I'M NOT your possession, Raul.*'

Raul watched her and wished he'd had the foresight to send out for some clothes for her. At least then he might have stood a chance of being able to concentrate.

He'd never considered a plain white shirt to be sexy, but Faith managed to turn it into something that could have become a top seller in a sex shop.

It wasn't the shirt, he decided grimly, it was the woman.

Faith would have looked sexy dressed in her grandmother's clothes.

And she was looking straight at him, her green eyes wide and intelligent. '*Talk* to me, Raul,' she urged softly, all the fight suddenly leaving her. '*Tell* me why you're thinking like this. Is there something I need to know? Did someone hurt you? *Did someone betray your trust?*'

She'd changed tactic in mid-fight but this alternative, gentler assault was infinitely more deadly than the fierce blast of her temper.

She was getting close. Too close. Closer than any woman had ever dared tread before.

'We've been talking non-stop,' he said coldly, retreating mentally and physically from the question he saw in her eyes.

'Maybe we haven't been talking about the right things.'

Swiftly, he sidestepped an issue he had no intention of exploring further. '*You* betrayed my trust.'

'No.' She shook her head slowly. '*Why* would you even think that?'

'Because you went to astonishing lengths to drag me into this marriage.'

'That is *not* what happened!'

'Then what did happen, Faith? Why are we standing here, as husband and wife, because I sure as hell don't know!' His words thickened, his usually faultless accent tinged with a hint of his South American heritage.

She stood in front of him and he could actually see her slim legs shaking. In fact she was shaking so badly that for a moment he wondered whether she might actually collapse. Her face had lost every last hint of colour and she looked as though she were in shock. 'We're here because I thought it was what you wanted. You proposed, Raul. You asked me to marry you.'

'Because you gave me no other option! Have you listened to anything I've said over the past ten months?' With a supreme effort of will, he kept his voice level even though the temptation to vent his wrath was extreme. 'Right from the beginning I made it clear to you—no marriage, no babies. If that's what you had planned then you should have been with another man.'

But even as he uttered the words he knew them for a lie. *He would never have let her go to another man.*

'I didn't have anything planned. I didn't *plan* any of this!' Some of her spirit returned. 'I came to your wretched *estancia* because the job was interesting and I wanted to see something of South America. All you were to me was a name. A guy who knew about horses!'

Watching her trembling and shaking in front of him, Raul frowned. 'Calm down.' She looked impossibly fragile and he watched with a mixture of concern and exasperation as she grew more and more agitated, her slender hands clasping and unclasping by her sides.

'Don't tell me to calm down! How can I possibly calm down when you're accusing me of planning as though I'm some sort of s-s—' she stumbled over the word '—scheming woman, out to trap you. I'm *not* scheming. I never planned or plotted. I had an accident! It happens to millions of women every day! And it wasn't just my fault! You were there, too! You're very quick to blame me, but I wasn't alone in this. I didn't have sex by myself. You were there, Raul, every time. You were there in our bed every night. You were there in the shower, in the stables, in your office, in the fields—wherever I was, you were. *I didn't do this by myself!*'

Her passionate diatribe conjured up images of such disturbing clarity that it took him a moment to formulate a response. 'You assured me that you were protected.'

'Well, it seems that nothing is foolproof. I've thought about it and thought about it.' Faith swallowed. 'I was sick, if you remember. I picked up that bug when we spent the night in that hotel outside Cordoba, when you were looking at a horse. I didn't even think of it at the time, but it was probably enough—'

He digested that information in silence. 'It's history now.'

'No, it isn't history. I can't be with a man who would think that badly of me!'

'All marriages hit sticky patches.'

'But not within hours of the ceremony! I hate you, Raul.' The tears spilled down her cheeks and she started to sob. Not delicate, controlled sobs designed to win a man round, but tearing, anguished sobs that seemed to place great strain on her slender frame. 'I hate you for not believing me, I hate you for marrying me when that wasn't what you really wanted, but most of all I really, *really* hate you for not caring that I lost the baby.'

Raul swore fluently and stepped towards her but she held up a hand to stop him.

'Don't come near me,' she choked. 'Don't you *dare* touch me or I'll injure you.'

He stiffened. 'You're obviously distressed—'

'And you are the reason for that distress! Make up your mind, Raul. You can't accuse me of lying and manipulating one minute and then offer to support me the next. When I told you that I'd lost the baby—*that* was when I needed your support.'

Her voice was thickened and clogged with tears. 'But what did you do? You accused me of having become pregnant on purpose to trap you into marriage. I didn't just lose the baby, I lost *you* because I realised then that I couldn't be with a man who would think me capable of something like that.'

'What was I supposed to think?' Infuriated by her totally unjust accusations, Raul felt his own tension levels soar.

'*You were supposed to think that I wouldn't have done that to you.* To us! That was what you were supposed to think.' Her face was streaked with tears but for some reason she didn't look pathetic or sorry for herself, just angry and passionate and very, very beautiful. 'I know you find it hard to show your feelings, but I *assumed* you loved me. I assumed you cared about me. It didn't occur to me to even question that because I thought we were happy together. So at the time, all I was really thinking about was the baby and how sad I was.'

Raul turned away and raked his fingers through his hair. 'It might have helped if you'd told me about the miscarriage *before* the wedding.'

'Well if I'd known how jaded and cynical you

are then perhaps I would have done, although goodness knows when! You arrived five minutes before the ceremony! If I'd talked about it then I would have broken down and I thought it would be bad for your image to be seen marrying a woman who was sobbing.'

'Faith—'

'Answer me honestly, Raul.' Her voice trembled and shook with emotion. 'Why did you propose to me? If you were truly so against marriage, *why* did you propose? If you remember, when I first discovered I was pregnant I told you that I did not expect you to marry me.'

'Yes, that was clever.'

'It wasn't clever! It was how I felt.' Increasingly agitated, Faith paced across the floor, her back to him as if she couldn't bear to look him in the eye. 'It was bad enough finding myself pregnant and knowing that you were going to blame me for that. Do you know how much courage it took to tell you I was pregnant? Do you know?' She turned, her eyes flashing. 'I could have vanished into the sunset and brought your baby up on my own, but I didn't do that because I decided that it wasn't right or honest. I decided that it wouldn't be fair to you.'

Raul stilled, black clouds from his past rolling towards him like a deadly storm. 'I would not have wanted you to do that,' he said hoarsely, sliding a finger round the neck of his shirt in an attempt to ease his breathing. 'I wouldn't have allowed that.' *Never.*

'Why not? If you're really so allergic to the thought of parenthood, then that would have been a perfectly reasonable option to consider.'

Not for him. Ruthlessly battling to rein in emotions that he hadn't experienced for years, Raul rubbed his fingers over his temples in the hope that touch might erase the memories. Not now. He wasn't going to think about this now. And not later, either. It was gone. Done. Finished.

'I'm *trying* to understand you, Raul.' Her eyes glittered like jade. 'And you're not helping.'

He inhaled deeply. 'When you told me that you were pregnant, I did *not* react badly.'

'You stood there, looking as though you'd been shot through the head at close range.' She turned away from him and he saw her chest rise and fall under the soft fabric of his shirt. She looked traumatised, fragile and desperately upset. 'What is going on here, Raul? Is this some sort of billionaire hang-up? Is that it? Woman gets pregnant so it must be because she wants your money?'

Raul watched her in tense silence. Their relationship was in shreds around them and he had no idea how to fix it because he'd never actually bothered fixing a relationship before. If it wasn't right, it ended. Simple as that.

So why wasn't he ending this one? 'You need to calm down—'

'*Stop* telling me to calm down! I don't feel calm. I'm angry, Raul. Angry with you. And angry with myself for believing that we had something special. It was bad enough telling you that I was pregnant, but I reassured myself that our relationship was strong enough to take it. We loved each other, or so I thought. I really believed that we'd weather this and make it work.' Her voice faltered and she gave a tiny intake of breath. 'And then I lost it.' That last statement was an anguished gasp and Raul felt his own tension rocket and every muscle in his body tensed in readiness for more female tears.

'Why didn't you tell me? I called you that night,' he reminded her. 'I called you every night I was away on business. You had ample opportunity.'

'I just couldn't do it over the phone...' Her

voice faded to a whisper and she dropped back onto the sofa as if her legs had lost their strength. 'How do you do that? I don't know—I mean, should I have said, "How was your day, dear? By the way, I lost the baby"?'

'Faith—'

'I was *devastated* and you hate emotional scenes, you know you do. Look at you now—you're standing there thinking to yourself, "I hope she doesn't cry again. Once was enough."'

'That isn't true,' Raul lied swiftly but her soft, derisive laugh told him that he'd been less than convincing. He paced to the furthest end of the living room although why, he didn't really know. There was already an enormous gulf between them. Physically and emotionally they were as far apart as it was possible for two people to be.

'It's all irrelevant. What matters now is that we're married. And we have to find a way of moving forward from here.' He thought of the past year and the passion they'd shared. He'd loved the fact that she hadn't known who he was at their first meeting. Loved the fact that the chemistry between them had been raw and explosive and *nothing* to do with who he was.

And even when she'd discovered his identity, it hadn't changed her. She'd continued to be herself, challenging him constantly without guarding what she said. Surrounded by people who deferred to him, he'd found Faith a revelation. *And then there had been the sex.*

'Raul, it's over.'

'You're my wife, Faith. I want you back in my bed.'

She gaped at him. 'You *have* to be kidding.'

Taken aback by her less than enthusiastic response to his statement, Raul frowned. 'Every relationship goes through rocky patches.'

'This isn't a rocky patch, Raul, it's a mountain range!'

'I told you earlier that there wouldn't be a divorce.'

'I assumed you didn't mean it.'

'We were good together.'

'At sex. You're just being ridiculously possessive and macho. You're doing it again—that whole Argentine-man thing.' Her face was terrifyingly pale and she rose to her feet so suddenly that her body swayed.

With a sharp frown, Raul stepped towards her but before he could reach her her legs gave way and she sank to the floor, unconscious.

* * *

'These things happen after a head injury, but it's important that she avoids any unnecessary stress.'

Faith woke to find herself lying on the bed with a doctor hovering over her and groaned. *Not more doctors.*

'She really needs peace and quiet,' he was saying and Faith struggled to sit up.

'What happened?'

'You fainted,' the man said calmly and Faith frowned.

'I never faint.'

The man closed his bag. 'You can't expect to return to full health immediately. You need to take it gently.'

'I intended to take her back to the *estancia* tomorrow.' Raul's face was strained and the doctor nodded.

'It's only a short drive. She will be fine, I'm sure. But you need to remember that a miscarriage followed by a head injury—it's a lot for anyone to cope with.' He picked up his medical bag and left the room with Raul.

A few moments later Raul was back, a wary expression on his handsome face.

Faith lay still, just watching him. 'Why are

you staring at me like that? I'm not about to break in two.'

'The doctors think that the reason you're so emotional could be because of the miscarriage,' he said tightly. 'They think you should be encouraged to talk about it.'

'Talk?' Faith gave a weak laugh. 'They don't know you very well, do they? Now I understand why you're looking green around the gills. You're afraid I suddenly want to expose you to my inner feelings. Relax, Raul. I wouldn't discuss it with you if you were the last person on earth.'

He absorbed the insult without attempt at retaliation, his face grim as he studied her in silence. Then he dropped something into her lap.

Faith looked at it and her heart stopped dead.

'It's your wedding ring,' he said in a harsh voice. 'The wedding ring you threw at me only two hours after I'd placed it on your finger. Put it on. You're mine and don't ever forget it again.'

Remembering how she'd felt when she'd removed it, Faith felt the lump return to her throat. 'Do you know something?' she said in a shaky voice that didn't sound like her own. 'Until I met you, I could never understand why a woman would be so stupid as to cry over a man. And here I am, doing exactly that.'

'Put it on. You should never have taken it off your finger.'

'You should never have put it on my finger, feeling the way you felt.' She took the ring in her hand but didn't put it on.

'I did not intentionally upset you.'

'Don't say that, Raul, because if you've achieved this level of devastation without even trying, I don't even want to think about what you might manage if you really applied yourself.'

'I'm willing to admit that I was thinking of my feelings rather than yours.' His surprising admission left her speechless and he sat on the edge of the bed, his dense lashes lowered as he studied her. 'I *am* trying.'

'Are you?'

'I'm here.'

'Claiming your "possession"; wasn't that the word you used? Give me one reason why I should even think about putting this ring back on my finger.'

'Because you love me.'

His arrogant statement rocked her to the core. *Did she love him?* Was she really such a poor judge of character? 'Go away, Raul. You heard the doctor—I'm not supposed to be subjected to any stress and you definitely fall under the category of stress.'

'You love me, Faith.' His voice was dangerously intimate and she glared at him angrily but the anger was as much directed towards herself as him. She shouldn't be listening to him. She shouldn't be giving him air-time.

'Do you want to have to explain to the doctor why I've collapsed again?'

His response to that was to take her cold fingers in his warm, strong grip and slide the ring onto her finger in a decisive gesture. '*Don't* take it off again. And now I want you to tell me how you feel.'

'No, you don't.' She gave a hollow laugh. 'Trust me, you really don't want to go there. And anyway, we both know that you would sooner eat glass than discuss my feelings.'

'That is *not* true.' His fingers tightened on hers. 'Whatever you may think, I do care about you. The doctors say you need to talk about the miscarriage. I explained that the pregnancy was an accident, but they didn't seem to think that would make any difference to the emotional impact.'

'And that was news to you?' Her voice shook as the pain shot through her. 'You think that made any difference to my feelings? Do you think that made it hurt any the less?'

'I don't know.' His tone was cool and detached. 'I have no experience in this area.' And he hadn't wanted any experience; that much was obvious from every taut, stiff line of his powerful frame.

'I don't know why we're talking about this.'

'Because the doctors seem to think it might help you. Did it hurt, physically?' His voice was gruff and she stared at the ceiling, feeling as though the bottom was dropping out of her world, yet again.

'Raul, I really don't—'

'Talk to me!'

'Why? So that you can watch me unravel like a ball of wool?' Her strangled laugh was like a warning bell, indicating that the volumes of tension building inside her were reaching danger levels. 'Is that what you're asking?'

'Dios mío, do *not* attack me when I am trying to help! *Tell* me what is in your head.'

His hand rested close to hers and the fact that her own fingers tingled with the need to touch shocked her. He wasn't capable of giving comfort, so why was she hoping for it? 'I'm angry. That's how I feel.'

'*Sí*, that much I can see for myself,' he growled. 'What else?'

'Sad,' she whispered, curling her fingers into the soft duvet that covered her. 'And guilty. Because I was so worried about what the baby would do to you and to us. It didn't occur to me that I might lose it. And now I'm wondering—'

'It was *not* your fault.' The fact that he'd read her mind surprised her because she hadn't thought he was capable of being so connected with her thoughts.

'You don't know that. It feels as though it is.' Her voice was clogged with tears. 'Perhaps that baby knew that it had stirred up a hornet's nest between us. Perhaps it knew, Raul.'

'You are torturing yourself for no reason.'

'You wanted to know how I feel. I'm telling you. I feel guilty. Sad. Disappointed. Angry with you.' She swallowed painfully and her voice dropped to a whisper. 'And empty. Really, really empty. Because I've lost something that was part of me. Part of us. And I know it wasn't planned, but once I found out about it I just wanted it.' It was too much. Letting a tiny drop of emotion escape was dangerous when so much of it was bottled up.

'You always were maternal. I watched you delivering foals and I knew then that you were trouble.' His tone was gruff and she knew he was acknowledging what they'd both known: *that this was always going to be an enormous issue between them.*

'I didn't think it would be a problem,' she admitted hoarsely. 'I had no plans to settle down and get married. Children were something in the far-distant future so when you told me that wasn't what you wanted, I suppose it just didn't really seem relevant. We were having fun and we were happy. That was what mattered.'

'The problem was always there.'

'Only if you were thinking in terms of marriage and a future, and I wasn't.' Her fingers tightened on the duvet. 'I didn't see it as a problem.'

'You mean you hoped I would wake up one morning longing to be a father.'

'No, I mean I wasn't thinking about parenthood. I was just enjoying our relationship.'

His gaze didn't shift from her face. 'And now?'

'Well, I don't think this is the most fun we've ever had together, if that's what you're asking me,' she croaked and he rose to his feet and gave her a long, speculative look that made her stomach tumble and turn.

'I never wanted to hurt you.'

'Raul, don't—'

'I love being with you.'

It was as close to a declaration of love as he'd ever come, and for a moment she couldn't breathe. Afraid that she'd make a fool of herself, she squeezed her eyes tightly shut. 'Getting soppy on me, Raul?'

'Perhaps.'

She gave a soft moan of agony. 'It's easier to deal with you when you're angry and unreasonable. Why are you doing this to me now, when it's too late for us?'

'It isn't too late.'

If she'd thought she was confused before, she was doubly so now. 'How can you claim to care about me when you *hurt* me?'

'If I didn't care, I wouldn't be here now.' He didn't try and touch her but somehow that made his simple statement all the more compelling and she screwed her eyes tightly shut.

'We make each other miserable.'

'Until we married we were extremely happy

together.' His voice was tense. 'We need to put all this behind us and move on. Concentrate on our relationship.'

'I can't just put it behind me—'

'So what are you going to do?' His voice was brutal. 'Carry on like this? Walking under cars, winding yourself up to a state of such anxiety that you pass out?'

Numb, she looked at him. 'What do you *want* from me?'

'You,' he said simply. 'Back in my bed where you belong.' It was such a typically macho declaration that she closed her eyes tightly, hating herself for even considering it.

'You hurt me, Raul.'

'And you hurt me.'

Accepting that as a truth, she opened her eyes. 'You seriously expect to carry on with our marriage?'

'You are getting upset again and you are very pale. Last time we talked about this you collapsed on the floor at my feet,' he bit out. 'So we're going to leave the subject until you're feeling stronger. In the meantime you'll just have to accept the fact that we're married and that we're staying that way. We're not going to talk about this again, now.' He turned and strode towards the bedroom door. 'Get some rest. I need to do some work.'

Too exhausted and drained to argue with him further, Faith collapsed against the pillows, feeling as though she'd been run over all over again. Now what?

Part of her was worried that she felt so lousy, but another part of her was far too distracted by her relationship with Raul to pay much attention to her own health.

Why was he so determined that they should stay married when it was clear that he'd only married her because of the baby?

What hope was there for them?

And then she remembered just how good their relationship had been—how much she loved him.

Just how much could a person forgive?

Did she dare try to make their marriage work?

If she chose that path, how much pain lay ahead of her?

Her head full of doubts and questions, she couldn't relax or lie still so she slid out of bed and padded on bare feet out of the bedroom and into the living room.

Raul was sprawled on the sofa, his eyes closed.

His shirt was undone at the collar, his sleeves were rolled up and dark stubble emphasised the lean, hard lines of his handsome face.

He looked exhausted and Faith felt her heart twist. Five minutes earlier she'd wanted to slap him. Now she wanted to put her arms round him and hug him.

Confused and infuriated with herself, she was about to turn away when his eyes opened and he saw her.

For a moment they just stared at each other and she felt her cheeks burn as she saw the sudden flare of heat in his eyes. Every feminine part of her exploded with awareness and she knew from the sudden tension in his shoulders that he was experiencing the same powerful reaction.

Acknowledging the strength of the force that drew them together, he gave a cynical laugh. 'Complicated, isn't it?'

'Yes.' It would have been foolish to pretend that she didn't know what he was talking about. She stood for a moment, trying to catch her breath, needing to speak and not knowing how to say what needed to be said. 'I didn't mean to force your hand. I thought we were good together.'

'We were.'

'But—you never would have wanted marriage.'

'No.' His face was closed, uncommunicative and she looked at him with mounting frustration.

'Why? If a relationship is good, marriage just makes it better.'

His laugh hurt more than any harsh words. 'And we're a case in point, are we?'

'Is there anything left between us?'

His answer was to rise to his feet and stride across to her. Without bothering to speak, he closed his fingers around her wrist, pulled her hard against him. 'How can you ask that, when this thing between us has been choking us since the day we met?'

Without giving her a chance to reply, he brought his mouth down on hers.

As kisses went, this one wasn't gentle but she didn't even care. It was an explosion of mutual need, an acknowledgement of the passion and chemistry that kept both of them locked together when external forces might have driven them apart.

Excitement swamped her, her head swam with a rush of dizzying pleasure and she would have slid to the floor if he hadn't wrapped his arms around her.

They kissed with desperation, their mouths

locked together in a furious, reckless urgency that exploded away the flimsy barriers that had been erected between them.

It was only when his hand touched her breast that Faith regained sufficient mental ability to realise what she was doing.

'We can't fix problems with sex,' she groaned, but the erotic skill of his mouth stole the words and her body shivered against his. 'Raul, this is just too complicated to solve in this way—'

'Life is complicated,' he muttered, his lips trailing down the line of her jaw. 'In real life, people are complicated and they behave in complicated ways.'

'You didn't think about my feelings.'

He lifted his head and looked at her. 'Both of us were guilty of that.' His return shot scored a direct hit and she stiffened.

'With hindsight I can see that I should have told you I'd lost the baby, but my reasons for not telling you *were* unselfish.' Her stumbled admission received no more response than a raised eyebrow and a careless lift of his shoulders.

'If there's one thing that the last few months has proved, it's that neither of us knows the other as well as we thought.' His handsome face was grim. 'That is common. It's the reason that so many marriages end in divorce. We can change that, Faith. But not if you run.'

She looked at him, torn by indecision, her head full of problems and questions. Logic told her to do one thing, her heart another.

'If I stay, I won't let you hurt me again,' she warned in a voice that shook with emotion. 'Don't *ever* hurt me again.'

CHAPTER SEVEN

IT FELT strange being back when she'd thought she'd never see the place again.

Faith sat in silence in the back of the limousine as it drove through the ornate iron gates that guarded the entrance of the *estancia*.

She couldn't quite believe she was actually here.

What if she was making the biggest mistake of her life by giving their marriage another chance?

She sighed and stared out of the window. Obviously she was just a pushover for a big, arrogant South American male.

But she knew it was more than that.

She loved him and she couldn't just switch that off.

And she loved Argentina.

Despite the nagging ache in her head and the dull feeling of nausea in her stomach, part of her felt lighter just for being here. After the noise and bustle of Buenos Aires, the wide open space of the pampas was a welcome refuge.

It was an incomparably beautiful place.

Grassland stretched into the distance and a herd of Criollo ponies galloped and bucked, manes and tails flying, clearly enjoying the freedom of the wide, open planes.

As the car purred along the tree-lined avenue and curved round the final bend, Faith held her breath in expectation. Raul had once told her how he'd bought the place piece by piece.

He'd shown her photographs and she'd barely recognised the tumbledown, dusty buildings.

The ranch had been restored to its former colonial glory and now the dusky-pink stone walls of the main residence were covered in tumbling bougainvillea, the colours so bright that at a glance it seemed as if someone had gaily splashed paint against the walls. Three perfectly manicured polo lawns were bordered by pristine white fences and in another field a herd of exquisitely beautiful horses galloped and pranced, the quality of their bloodline indisputable.

Faith's eyes slid to the row of expensive cars parked in the far corner of the immaculate yard.

Money, money and more money…

Raul had barely spoken during the journey, instead working on his laptop and fielding a never-ending series of calls, the subject of which had revolved around the purchase of a neighbouring *estancia*.

'You're buying more land?'

A strange expression flickered across his face and she sensed immediately that this was one deal he didn't intend to discuss. 'Are you making small talk or are you suddenly interested in the nature of my business?'

Four days had passed since they'd first arrived in Buenos Aires and apart from that one kiss, he hadn't touched her. Once he'd put the ring back on her finger, he'd turned his attention to work, dividing his time between the phone and the computer. The only time they'd met up had been for dinner by the pool, a stiff, uncomfortable affair for Faith, an opportunity to refuel for Raul. He'd never lingered, instead opting to return to the room he used as an office. His desk faced the glass window and she'd caught glimpses of him lounging in his leather chair, long, muscular legs stretched out in front of him as he'd given hell to the person on the end of the phone.

Faith had immediately retreated to her favourite place, the cosy sofa that took advantage of the same view that Raul enjoyed from his office. She'd cradled a book in her lap, but hadn't read a single word. Instead she'd stared out of the window, her thoughts far removed from the printed page of a book.

She'd always thought that the physical side of their relationship was the one area where they would never have a problem. But apart from that one, searing kiss, Raul hadn't touched her. When he'd slept, which wasn't often, he'd slept in the spare room and she hadn't questioned him because she hadn't wanted to appear insecure.

But she couldn't help wondering *why*.

Was it because her hair was short?

Was it because she'd lost weight?

Halfway through her second day in his apartment, a delivery had arrived for her and she'd opened the various boxes and discovered an entire wardrobe. Dresses, shoes, casual wear, underwear, nightwear—the fact that it had been lacking nothing was a testament to Raul's experience of women but she'd tried not to think about that as she'd riffled her way through the various boxes.

If she was seriously going to give their marriage another go, then she needed to stop thinking like that.

So now, as she arrived at the *estancia*, she was wearing a cool summer dress in soft, muted shades of green and a simple pair of sandals. Lifting her hand to her head, she fingered her hair self-consciously and he caught the gesture and gave a frown.

'Don't. I like it.'

It was the first compliment he'd paid her since he'd stormed into the hospital on that first day and Faith gazed at him in surprise. 'You do?'

'Yes.' He gave a smile that was faintly mocking. 'You look like a pixie.'

'Oh.' She wanted to ask whether he found pixies sexy but then realised that she already knew the answer to that question. *Obviously not, since he hadn't been near her for the past four days.*

And she was relieved about that, she told herself firmly, because she wasn't ready to make love with him yet. Yes he was impossibly sexy, but for her it was more complicated than that. Her feelings were bruised and damaged and before she committed herself emotionally, she needed to know that he cared about her.

She needed him to show it.

Maria, the housekeeper, hurried across the courtyard towards them and Raul gave her a warm smile.

'*Buenos dias*, Maria, *qué tal*?'

Wistfully remembering a time when he'd smiled at her with the same warmth, Faith also greeted the older lady and then followed her towards the luxurious Beach House that was Raul's private residence.

He could have lived in the thirty-two-roomed *estancia*, but instead he'd turned it into his corporate headquarters, complete with suites of rooms for entertaining and overnight guests. For his own personal use, he'd chosen the privacy and intimacy of the Beach House, well away from the busy commercial world of the *estancia*.

The first time she'd seen it, Faith had been unable to believe that such paradise actually existed.

It was hidden from the main house by trees and fencing, and opened onto a private beach so breathtakingly idyllic that the world outside seemed not to exist and the only sound was the gentle hiss of waves breaking onto the perfect curve of white sand.

'Everything is ready for you,' Maria told Raul

as she opened the door for them. 'Just as you instructed.'

Dragging her gaze from the sea, Faith gave a gasp of surprise. The elegant Beach House was filled with the scent of flowers and someone had obviously given a great deal of thought to their return. On the table, a basket was piled high with exotic fruit and a bottle of vintage champagne lay chilling in an ice bucket.

'All Raul's idea,' Maria said, her approval evident in her smile. 'Newlyweds deserve something a little special.'

Faith felt the colour pour into her cheeks. Just what did Raul's staff know about the last few weeks? Had they guessed about the state of their marriage?

Clearly keen to leave them alone, Maria said something else in Spanish to Raul and then left the Beach House, closing the door behind her.

Faith glanced around her, her mouth dry. 'You asked for this?'

'To prove that I *am* capable of being thoughtful,' he drawled softly, reaching for the bottle of champagne and tugging out the cork.

Faith was on the verge of pointing out the fact that she would have preferred a conversation, but decided that this wasn't the time to dent the atmosphere.

'What do your staff know about the last few weeks?'

'I have no idea.' Raul poured the glistening liquid into two glasses. 'I'm not in the habit of discussing my personal life with the staff.'

'Well, you must have given them some explanation for the fact we haven't been living here.'

'Why?' Genuinely puzzled by her question, Raul unbuttoned his shirt and walked towards the bedroom. 'I have no idea what they think and I couldn't care less. And neither should you.'

They were *so* different, Faith thought helplessly, watching as he slid the shirt from his shoulders. 'Actually I *do* care what they think,' she muttered and he gave a wolfish smile.

'Then learn not to, because most people in this world are not that generous-spirited. If you really want to know, they're thinking you're obviously extremely hot in bed or there is no way you'd be wearing that ring on your finger.'

She flushed to the roots of her hair. 'Oh.'

His smile widened and he walked into the bedroom without giving her a chance to respond and she stared after him with exasperation.

There was so much that they still needed to talk about.

So much that she needed to know. 'Raul?' She followed him into the bedroom. 'We can't carry on like this. The past few days, you've been driving yourself into the ground, working until you're ready to drop. I don't know whether it's pressure of your business or whether you're just avoiding this thing between us, but we *have* to talk. Not rows and accusations, but *really* talk. It isn't going to go away and we can't just pretend it never happened.'

He stilled. Then he turned slowly and their eyes locked.

And that one, powerful, sizzling look was all it took.

Her stomach knotted with almost unbearable tension and she felt every nerve ending in her body tingle and buzz with shocking awareness. Her breasts tightened and deep in her stomach something burned, hot and dangerous as desire engulfed her.

He felt it too, she knew he did because she saw the betraying glitter in his sexy, dark eyes and the sudden flare of colour on his high cheekbones.

The attraction enveloped them like an invisible force, burning everything in its path like a forest fire, drawing them relentlessly towards an outcome that both of them had been fiercely resisting.

He strode back towards her and pushed her back against the wall. His body trapped hers as he took her face in his hands, forcing her to meet his burning gaze.

'I think we're way past talking, Faith,' he said huskily, all sexually confident male as his thumb traced a sensual path across her cheek. 'All we've done for the past few days is talk and it's been driving me crazy.'

'But we haven't solved anything,' Faith gasped, turning her head to try and escape his agonisingly skilful touch. But they both knew it was a losing battle.

'Frustrating, isn't it?' He gave a harsh laugh and then lowered his head and drew his mouth along the line of her jaw where his thumb had been, sending the heat between them soaring higher still. 'You think it was easy to let you sleep alone, *cariño*? You think I found that easy? *A man like me?*'

It hadn't been easy for him? 'I didn't think about it,' she lied, her voice barely audible as it became harder and harder to speak. 'You hurt me so badly, sex was the last thing on my mind.'

He gave a cynical laugh. 'If only that were true, life would be a great deal less complicated. Unfortunately for you and I, chemistry seems to override common sense every time. You were thinking about it as much as I was. I could see it in your eyes every time you sat in that chair *not* reading that book on your lap.'

'That's not true,' she moaned, but the smouldering glitter in his eyes told her that the lie had been a waste of breath.

'You want honesty between us?' he breathed. 'Then let's have honesty. I have wanted you for every second of the day and night since the first time I met you and nothing has changed that.'

His words affected her so deeply that there wasn't a single part of her body that didn't react. 'So why did you let me sleep alone?' She tried to remind herself that it wasn't supposed to matter, that she wasn't supposed to care any more, but it was as if her body was tuned to respond only to his. 'I assume you were punishing me?'

'Punishing myself,' he said huskily, his hand curving over her bottom in an unmistakably possessive gesture that rocked her to the very core.

'The doctor told me that you were to avoid all stress. From the disapproving look in his eyes, I assumed he considered me to be the cause of your stress. I stayed away from you and I can tell you that doing so has caused havoc with *my* stress levels.'

His body was hard against hers and it was impossible to think. 'I wondered whether— You told me I was thin…' Overwhelmed by his sexuality, she tried to catch a breath, hating herself for giving voice to her very female insecurities. 'And you keep looking at my hair—you don't find me attractive any more.'

'No, you're right.' His voice was thickened as he hauled her closer still. 'I don't find you at all attractive.' But his words were loaded with self-mockery and she gasped as her body encountered the unmistakable evidence of his shockingly powerful arousal.

'We really shouldn't do this.' Faith's body was no longer her own. 'This is going to make things worse,' she moaned and he captured the sound with his mouth, the fierce demand of his kiss plunging her past the point of no return.

'Worse?' he murmured in a thickened voice. 'How in heaven's name can the situation between us be any worse, *cariño*? I'm made of flesh and blood, not stone, and the past few weeks have been intolerable.'

She tried to hang on to her sanity. 'You thought I became pregnant on purpose—'

'*Dios mío*, why are you bringing that up now? It doesn't matter any more! *This* is the only thing that matters.' His hands cupped her face and he kissed her until physical sensations completely overwhelmed her. She reached for his shoulders, excited and terrified by the sexual craving that threatened to consume her.

Even knowing that there was going to be even greater pain ahead, Faith was unable to do anything except respond. She was so lost in a wild maelstrom of sensation that she didn't even realise that he'd unzipped her dress until it slid to the floor, leaving her standing in her under-wear. She clutched at his shoulders, feeling the hard swell of male muscle under her fingers, re-velling in the strength and power of his body.

He was pumped up and aroused and she gave a choked cry as his hand cupped her breast through the thin, silken fabric and he stroked her with skilled clever fingers.

The delicious friction of his thumbs over her

nipples sent intense excitement shooting through her body and it would have been impossible not to respond. She arched against him in desperate invitation, feeling the heavy, rigid thrust of his arousal and the immediate explosion of heat deep in the core of her femininity.

He kept his mouth on hers, his kiss demanding and shockingly intimate, but all the time his fingers teased her breasts, driving her wild. Only when her breasts ached and throbbed with almost agonising sensation did he slide his clever, confident hands down her shivering, quivering body.

Mindless and desperate, Faith slid one foot up his leg and he caught her thigh in his hand, lifting her leg higher and wider, exposing her to his touch. Once, such a wanton position would have brought a blush to her cheeks but she was too aroused to think about modesty or behaviour. The response of her body was outside her own control and as she felt his knowing fingers slide over the thin fabric of her panties she shuddered and pressed towards his hand. Only a layer of thin, flimsy silk lay between them but it was too much of a barrier and she gave a moan and shifted her hips, just desperate for him to touch her *there*.

But he didn't.

Instead he tormented them both by prolonging the moment that they craved so desperately, very much in control despite the hunger that consumed both of them.

Driven wild with excitement, her fingers slid downwards, reaching for him and he broke the kiss with a harsh groan as the flat of her hand brushed against his pulsing erection.

'Faith—'

Desperate and urgent, her fingers dealt with his zip, slid inside and encountered the warm throb of masculine power. Touching him so intimately, she felt an explosion of pure sexual need. He was so unashamedly male, so virile, that for a moment her heart seemed to beat double-time. She couldn't quite circle him with her hand and as usual she felt a flash of trepidation that he might be more of a man than she could handle.

'You're driving me wild, *cariño*,' he groaned and his hand moved again and this time he slid his fingers under the silken barrier that still protected her. The intimate stroke of his fingers was the touch she'd longed for and she whimpered his name, her eyes closing as his fingers slid deep, her damp, desperate body closing around him. She didn't know herself when she was with him. Didn't recognise the person she became. Devoured by sensation she was powerless to resist as his long clever fingers explored her with astonishing expertise. She felt the pressure build, felt her body race headlong towards completion and then he gently removed his hand and brought his mouth down on hers with punishing force.

His kiss made her so dizzy that she was only dimly aware of him lifting her, of him coiling her other leg around his hips. There was a brief moment of clarity when she felt the blunt tip of his arousal brush against her and then suddenly she felt a blind flash of panic and struggled against him. 'No, Raul. *No.*'

He froze, his breathing harsh, his body on the point of penetrating hers. 'No?' His voice was hoarse with disbelief, his entire frame straining with the tension of holding back. 'What do you mean, no?'

'We have to stop. Put me down!'

Two streaks of colour on his cheeks, Raul hesitated for a tense, pulsing moment and then lowered her gently and released her. Stepping away from her, he leaned both hands against the wall and breathed deeply, clearly struggling for control.

'Raul—'

'Don't.' His tone was raw and savage. 'Just give me a minute—'

Faith watched helplessly, not knowing what to do or say, her own body singing with unresolved passion. It didn't help that he was half-undressed, his bronzed back bared for her greedy gaze, his trousers riding low on his hips.

She closed her eyes with a groan because her only hope was not to look at him.

What was it about this man that made her forget herself every time?

Finally he drew in a breath and turned, his dark eyes burning with feverish intensity. 'So what was that all about?' His dark hair was tousled from the aggravated plunge of his fingers and he reached down and zipped his trousers with a purposeful movement. 'It was a joke or a punishment?'

'Neither.' Shivering and shaking, she stooped and retrieved her dress, holding it in front of her like a shield.

'Then *what*? You wanted it as badly as I did,' he said in a driven tone. 'So don't pretend that you didn't.'

'I'm not pretending anything.'

'So *why* did you stop?' His eyes were dark as

a winter night and Faith licked her lips, trying to ignore the fact that her entire body was suddenly alive with anticipation.

'Contraception,' she croaked, watching as his expression froze. 'For a man who doesn't want babies, you're extremely careless, do you know that?'

He stilled and a sudden silence screamed through the room.

'I am *not* careless.' His breathing suddenly shallow, he ran a hand over the back of his neck. 'Not usually. I did not intend to put you at risk— I forgot that you didn't use protection.'

And there it was, back again. This thing that lay between them. 'I *did* use protection,' she said flatly. 'But I stopped taking the Pill when I found out that I was pregnant. And I didn't start taking it again after I lost the baby.' She looked away from him but felt the tension levels rocket in the room.

'So, clearly that's something we need to address sooner rather than later.' His voice was rough, still laden with the passion that thickened the air and scraped along the edges of their nerve endings.

'No, we don't!' She took several steps backwards and found herself against the wall again. The same wall that just moments earlier she'd been pinned to under the weight of his body. 'We shouldn't even be *thinking* about sex when things are so complicated between us, Raul!'

'We have thought about nothing but sex since the first moment we met, *cariño*, and you know it.'

Faith wished there was a switch she could flick to turn off the responses of her body. *She didn't want to feel like this.* 'And that's our problem, isn't it?'

'Problem?' One dark eyebrow swooped upwards in sardonic appraisal. 'The fact that you are capable of satisfying me in the bedroom is the one thing that is absolutely *right* about our relationship. I certainly don't see it as a problem.'

His oblique reference to her abandoned response to him sent the colour flooding into her cheeks. 'You can't base a relationship on sex!'

'Never underestimate the importance of sex.'

Her heart rate doubled. 'I know it's important, but if sex is the only thing that is right about our relationship then we're doomed, Raul. A marriage is about trust and caring. We need to talk.'

Casting her a glance laden with hot-blooded volatility, Raul stepped back from her. 'If you want to talk, phone a girlfriend.' Simmering with unfulfilled passion and male hormones, he strode into the bedroom, leaving her staring after him in disbelief.

Stunned by the suppressed violence she sensed in him, Faith followed. 'You can't just walk out in the middle of a conversation just because you don't happen to like the subject matter—'

'*Dios mío*, not now!' With a low growl of impatience he turned, his hand on the bathroom door, his eyes burning into hers. 'You're a highly intelligent woman. Surely you're not so naïve that you can't see what is happening here? Either get dressed or get out.'

'But—'

'Faith—' The word was a deadly warning, as if he were holding on to control by a thread. 'I'm telling you now that if you stand there naked, I *will* finish what we started, contraception or no contraception. You will be back against that wall and this time I will *not* be stopping!'

Stunned by the appalling frankness of his words and the barely subdued violence of his reaction, she gave a little gasp. 'But there are so many issues between us—'

'At the moment I'm not interested in the issues, I'm just interested in sex.' Interpreting her shocked expression, he ran his hand over his face and swore long and fluently in Spanish. 'Does that make me shallow? Yes, probably, but I warned you before that I wasn't anyone's idea of a good catch. Remember that before you start trying to change me.'

'I don't want to change you,' Faith said honestly. 'I just want to understand what you're thinking.'

'No, I don't think you do, because what I'm thinking right now this moment,' he said in a silky tone, 'is that it is either a long, cold shower or you on that bed, naked with your legs wrapped around my waist. Your choice, *cariño*.'

'You're being shocking on purpose.'

'I'm being honest,' he said harshly. 'Because I thought that was what you wanted. Maybe now you'd like to rethink that particular demand, given that the truth of what is on a man's mind is so rarely what a woman wants to hear.'

Shaken to the core by the savagery in his voice, Faith backed towards the door. 'I'll—I'd better leave you alone. I'll see you later.'

'You certainly will and by then I will have addressed the issue of contraception so you can knock that particular excuse off your list.' He gave a humourless laugh and opened the bathroom door. 'In the meantime, we have guests for dinner. They arrive in two hours, and in order to concentrate on business I have to *not* be thinking about sex all the time. So this is what you're going to do. You're going to delve into that expensive wardrobe of yours and find something that covers you from head to toe. I want nothing showing.'

'Raul—'

'If necessary, sew two things together. Wear a coat! But I don't want to see cleavage or leg or so help me, Faith, I'll show you in public just how important sex is to me.' And with that rejoinder he strode into the sanctuary of the enormous bathroom and slammed the door firmly shut behind him.

Dios, *she was driving him wild.*

In the fierce grip of dark, primitive sexual need, Raul slammed the palm of his hand against the shower controls and sent fierce jets of freezing water cascading over his tense, throbbing body.

He closed his eyes, his jaw clenched, his teeth locked as he tried to let go of the tension. Every muscle in his body was pumped up and hard, the hormones coursing round his blood like a dangerous drug.

Litres of cold water sluiced over his heated, throbbing flesh and he stood there with grim determination until he finally acknowledged that he would develop pneumonia long before the desperate need in him died.

Unaccustomed to feeling sexual frustration, Raul leaned both hands against the wall and breathed deeply, trying to use his brain to calm the overwhelming need that tortured his body.

He hadn't intended to touch her like that; not then. What had happened to him? He, who prided himself on his control. He had more finesse than to indulge in mindless, animal sex and yet the facts spoke for themselves. The moment they'd been alone he'd had her up against the wall, his hand on her flesh…

He was behaving like a man possessed and he didn't know what had angered him most: the fact that she'd stopped him or the fact that he'd been so crazy for her that he hadn't given a single thought to anything except the immediate satisfaction of being inside her.

Not even the subject of contraception.

Never, with any other woman, would he have

forgotten contraception. It had been his mission, the single overriding fact that had governed the way he lived his life.

But with Faith…

Resigning himself to the fact that cold water was not going to cure his current affliction, he turned off the shower with another forceful punch of his hand and reached for a towel from the pile.

It didn't matter what she did, how she behaved, he wanted her more than any woman he'd ever met.

Acknowledging that fact with a growl of frustration, Raul wrapped the towel around his hips.

Marriage.

He'd avoided that institution all his life and yet somehow here he was, married.

And what had been a mutually satisfying relationship had been transformed into an emotional minefield that no sane man would attempt to negotiate.

He only had to think of her and the desire leapt inside him like a wild animal hunting its prey.

So now what? He mocked himself with the question. It was obvious that, like all women, she wanted him to talk. And given the look on her face when he'd given her a small taste of what was on his mind, he knew that if she really had access to his thoughts, their marriage would be over in a flash.

So perhaps now she'd learned her lesson and wouldn't risk asking him for his thoughts again, he thought grimly.

And he probably ought to do his bit for the relationship and prove that it wasn't all about sex. And that shouldn't be too hard. He might not believe in love, but he did enjoy the sparky, intellectual side of their relationship. He appreciated the fact that she was intelligent enough to challenge him in conversation. He was quite prepared to discuss the stock market, polo or any other subject that interested her.

In fact he was quite prepared to be thoughtful and caring, just as long as thoughtful and caring didn't involve an exchange of thoughts and feelings.

As long as they steered clear of that, their marriage should be fine.

CHAPTER EIGHT

FAITH stared at herself in the mirror, barely seeing her reflection.

What was she doing here? *How had she reached this point?*

She was an intelligent woman who could have been absorbed in her career, instead of which she was living at the whim of an extremely volatile billionaire, wondering whether she was wearing the right dress.

Impatient with herself, she turned sideways and took another look, wondering whether to go back and change into something different. Still on edge after their previous encounter, she had no idea how to handle Raul in his current mood.

They had entirely different ideas about marriage, she thought helplessly. *About life.*

For him, blistering sex was apparently enough.

Was that just his macho, South American genes coming into play?

Still shaken by the explosion of passion that had consumed both of them, Faith lifted a hand to her lips, still tasting the lick of his tongue and the heat of his kiss.

He'd been out of control. *Seriously* out of control. And so had she.

What had happened to her brain? What had happened to her ability to think clearly and logically?

Stopping had been the hardest thing she'd ever done, even harder than walking away from him because at the time, that had seemed the right thing to do.

And now? Did it seem right now?

She didn't know.

All she knew was that her body was buzzing and desire was racing round it like a dangerous drug.

With a groan of disbelief, she squeezed her eyes shut and tried to dispel the erotic images in her head. She had to stop him thinking about sex. And *she* had to stop thinking about sex. So, with that objective in mind, she'd been perfectly happy to comply with his command that she wear something discreet.

In the wardrobe he'd provided for her, she'd found a simple black dress that fell from a high neckline to the floor in a single sweep of soft fabric. She had no idea if it was too dressy for the evening ahead because he hadn't elaborated on what was expected of her. All she knew was that when she looked in the mirror, not one single part of her was on display except her arms.

Satisfied that she'd fulfilled his request, she walked into the living room on shaking legs. She was standing by the door looking across the beach, her stomach knotted in a turmoil of anticipation when she heard him enter the room.

Making sure that her defences were firmly in place, she took a slow breath and turned.

As always he exuded effortless style, his trousers superbly tailored to make the most of his physique, his jacket moulded to his wide shoulders. Tall, athletic and impossibly handsome, he looked every inch the wealthy and successful tycoon and the hint of arrogance in his bearing made her smile.

'I'm sure the other guy, whoever he is, will just give up on the spot when he sees you.' Her eyes slid over him. 'You look scary and intimidating when you dress for business, do you know that?'

'Appearance matters.'

'Spoken like a true Argentine male.'

His response to her light teasing was a careless shrug. 'I *am* an Argentine male, *cariño*. I have never denied that.'

But although she knew he was capable of using his looks when it suited him, she also knew that his success was due to his drive, energy and phenomenal intellect. Raul Vásquez was super-bright. His brain worked at twice the speed of most people's and he used his skills in that area to ruthless advantage, out-manoeuvering, out-negotiating.

He ran his eyes over her in silence and his eyes darkened. 'I told you not to wear anything provocative.'

Having been sure that her dress was perfect, Faith raised her eyebrows. 'This isn't provocative.'

'If you think that, then clearly you dressed without the aid of a mirror.'

Confused and exasperated, she glanced down at herself. 'You said no legs and no cleavage.'

'Your arms are showing.'

She lifted her head and looked at him. 'My *arms*?'

'Bare flesh, *cariño*,' he said huskily, a cool challenge in his eyes. 'If I see your arms, I can clearly imagine the rest of you. And if I'm imagining the rest of you, I'm not keeping my mind on business.'

Her heart had been behaving itself when he'd first walked into the room but suddenly it was bumping frantically against her chest. 'You're very basic.'

'Yes.'

'So don't take me with you. If I'm a distraction, then leave me here.'

He gave a faint smile. 'One of the benefits of having a wife,' he drawled, 'is being able to present her when the occasion demands it.'

'And does it?'

'This evening? Yes, it so happens that it does. Fetch a wrap,' he commanded, dragging his burning gaze from her body. 'And keep it on.'

'Perhaps you'd rather I wore a long coat?' Faith suggested acidly, using direct challenge as a method of disguising how deeply his words had affected her. *He wanted her with him.* Surely that was a positive sign?

He surprised her with a smile that was achingly sexy. 'Good idea. Coat and no dress. Just underwear.' His voice was deep and impossibly male. 'Later on I undo the coat and take you. And yes, this time you will have no excuse to stop.'

The vivid image his words created sent a burst of excitement through her stomach and it took her a moment to catch her breath. Trying desperately to conceal her reaction, Faith gritted her teeth. 'You're sex-mad, do you know that?'

'*Gracias.*'

She looked at him in exasperation. 'I didn't intend it as a compliment.' He was impossibly, arrogantly attractive and he shrugged his shoulders in a careless dismissal of her observation.

'Liking sex is a healthy and natural drive for a man. What's wrong with that?'

Wishing she'd never pursued this particular line of conversation, Faith drew in a long breath. 'Nothing. It's just—there are other things apart from sex. We could have a conversation.'

'*Sí.*' His eyes mocked her gently. 'Talking can be very intimate, I agree. Before and after sex.'

Now he was teasing her and the fact that he could succeed in making her hot and bothered even though she knew what he was doing, really irritated her. 'Talking isn't part of sex.'

'What do you think this is, if it isn't foreplay?' He murmured the words softly, his voice so sexy that she felt her limbs weaken. 'We are talking, yes, but we are both thinking about sex—'

'Raul, please don't do this.' She couldn't think clearly, not with his dark eyes suddenly alight with dangerous promise and his powerful body so achingly close.

'We both know what is coming later,' he purred. 'Each of us is thinking "how will it be?" and "can I wait that long?"' His normally fluent English seemed considerably less fluent than usual but there was no mistaking his meaning and his words were such an accurate assessment of her thoughts that she stilled, a bloom of colour touching her pale cheeks.

'That's not what I'm thinking,' she croaked and he gave a faint smile.

'Liar.'

She dragged her eyes from his. Only when she wasn't looking at him was there a chance that her brain would work. 'For a man with legendary intelligence, your goals are very shallow.'

'Would you be flattered if I climbed into bed with you and reached for a book?' He curved his hand around her waist, and she felt the instant response of her body.

'Do you ever think of anything other than sex?'

'*Sí*—sometimes I think of business.' He leaned forward and kissed her mouth, the hot slide of his tongue deliberately erotic. 'And now you need to stop distracting me or I am never going to get through the evening.'

'It isn't me, it's you—you started this.' But she was starting to feel the strain and he must have noticed because he slid his fingers under her chin and lifted her face to his.

'You're pale.'

She gave a careless shrug, trying not to betray everything that he made her feel. 'Jet lag. I'm tired.'

'No, it isn't that. I've seen you with more colour in your cheeks when you've been up all night with one of the horses.' He studied her closely, his scrutiny more than a little disturbing. 'Are you dizzy? Do you need a doctor?'

'No.' She didn't confess that she was just as wound up as he was. Every nerve ending in her body was reminding her that he was close by.

He watched her for a moment, and then increased the pressure of his hand and urged her towards the door. 'If this evening is too much for you, tell me and you can go back to bed.' He flashed her a confident, self-satisfied smile. 'You see how thoughtful and caring I can be?'

'Would that be an empty bed, or a bed with you in it?'

'We both know you would be mortally offended if I wasn't in it, *cariño*,' he purred, amusement in his eyes as he pulled her against him and stole a swift kiss from her parted lips. 'Then you would be accusing me of not finding you attractive, no?'

Tied into knots by his kiss, his smile and his words, she couldn't even respond.

She was a hopeless case, Faith thought weakly as she followed his direction and walked through the door on shaking legs. Desperately she tried to think about something, anything, other than him.

'These people we're meeting tonight—' she glanced at him briefly '—do I need to know anything about them? I don't want to say the wrong thing. Who are they?'

'They own land.' Raul took her hand in his and drew her close to him as they walked up the path that led from the Beach House to the main court-yard of the *estancia*. 'Land that I want.'

'You already own ten-thousand acres. Why would you want their land?'

'Why settle for less when you can have more?' But something flickered in the depths of his dark eyes and she had a feeling that there was more to this business deal than he was revealing.

'In other words, you have a good reason and you're not planning to share it with me.'

He laughed. 'I love the fact that you have a sharp brain.'

'Just as long as I don't use it,' Faith said tartly and his answer to that was to bring his mouth down on hers again, his kiss so impossibly skilled that the rest of her sharp rejoinder died in her brain.

'You taste good,' he murmured against her lips and she groaned and dragged her mouth away from his.

'You always *do* this to me.' She put her hands on his chest to steady herself, and then looked up at him. 'You're infuriating, do you know that? You use sex to shut me up.'

'*Not* true.' He bent his head and his mouth brushed her neck, that simple touch sufficient to send a thrill of excitement rushing through her.

'You're doing it again,' she gasped, wishing desperately that her body wasn't so responsive to his. 'Stop it, Raul.'

His mouth lingered, warm and full of promise. 'You want me to stop?' The erotic flick of his tongue fired her blood.

'No. Yes…' Sinking into a trance, Faith closed her eyes. 'I don't know. Where did you learn to do that?'

'I was born knowing,' he purred softly, but the twinkle in his eyes softened the arrogance of the statement. 'In Argentina, men know how to be men. And part of being a real man is being an incredible lover.'

'Your ego is enormous.'

His eyes darkened wickedly. 'That isn't my ego, *cariño*…'

All too aware of the strength and power of his arousal, Faith dragged herself out of his arms. 'All right, enough.' Flustered and shivering with desire, she held up a hand like a 'stop' sign. 'Just stand there and don't move for a minute.'

His gaze was slumberous and deadly. 'I love the fact that you're such a sexual woman.'

Faith gritted her teeth. 'I said *enough*! And no more kissing. I can't have a conversation while you're kissing me.'

One dark eyebrow swooped upwards in sardonic mockery. 'Precisely.'

Confused, her entire body buzzing, Faith glared at him. 'Do you know that you use sex to avoid every subject that is remotely difficult? You never talk about things that matter.' Her head was still reeling from the slow, seductive touch of his mouth and for a moment she wished that he wasn't quite so skilled in that area. If he had been less accomplished as a lover, she might have been able to concentrate on their relationship.

His beautiful eyes narrowed. 'I don't solve problems by committee.'

'I'm not a committee. I'm your wife.'

'*Sí*, and you knew the type of man you were marrying.' His tone hardened slightly but his gaze was still on her mouth. 'If you don't want me to think about sex, don't dress provocatively.'

'Well, what do I wear then, Raul? Tell me, because I certainly don't know.' Shaken by the depth of her own response to him, Faith smoothed the dress over her hips. 'You're staring at me.'

'Because I don't understand you,' he breathed. 'You would prefer that I don't find you attractive?'

'No, of course not. I'd just like there to be more to our relationship than sex.'

His thick lashes lowered slightly as he surveyed her. 'You don't like the fact that I want to make love to you day and night?'

His words made her stomach tumble and she dragged her gaze away from his, her breathing shallow. 'Of course I do. Any woman would, but—'

'So what is the problem?' The careless lift of his broad shoulders indicated that as far as he was concerned, there was nothing to solve.

'I feel as though I'm banging my head against a brick wall.'

'This is because of your accident perhaps.'

She turned to look at him, ready to thump him for that comment, and then she saw the twinkle in his eyes and realised that he was teasing her. 'You really like to live dangerously.'

His slow smile was impossibly sexy. 'Of course.'

She gritted her teeth. 'I hate you, do you know that?'

'*Sí, cariño.*' Ignoring her attempts to keep at a distance, he hauled her into his arms and brought her hips in direct contact with his. 'I know just how much you hate me. About as much as I hate you.' Sexual tension erupted with explosive force and Faith groaned a faint protest against his seeking mouth.

'I had a career before I met you,' she muttered, but he smothered her words with another assault on her lips, the skilled stroke of his tongue almost unbearably exciting as he kissed her until her head spun. Finally he lifted his head slowly and the look he gave her was one of pure, undiluted masculine satisfaction.

'I have no objection to your career. I'm very modern in my outlook.'

Faith would have laughed but she no longer had the energy. 'Modern? You make Neolithic men look progressive. Why am I with you? I used to have a brain.'

He smiled at that. 'You still have a brain, *cariño*.'

'So why am I standing here, kissing you?'

'Because I am the best at what I do,' Raul drawled with a trace of humour. 'And your brain is occupied in responding. I love your brain. Never think I don't.' He cupped her face possessively and looked into her eyes. 'And now, enough. We have guests arriving.'

And that was that, Faith thought helplessly. As far as he was concerned, that was the end of yet another conversation where he'd tied her in knots and revealed absolutely nothing about himself.

'If these negotiations really are important to you, then why are you taking me?' She turned away from him, unsure whether she was more annoyed with herself or him. 'I obviously just distract you.'

'I want you to be there.'

Resigning herself to the fact that she was unlikely to be given more of an explanation than that, Faith picked up her bag that she'd dropped on the floor when he'd kissed her. 'What role am I playing? Am I allowed to speak? Or do I pretend I've had a lobotomy?'

'You're my wife.' Raul smiled and that smile held such charm that for a moment Faith caught her breath.

'I hate it when you do that,' she muttered and his smile widened as he took her hand firmly in his.

'Do what?'

'You know what,' she said crossly, picking her way carefully up the path. 'You always use that smile of yours when you're losing an argument.'

'Lose?' He frowned at her. 'What is this "lose"? It isn't a word I know.'

'Very funny.' Faith pulled a face but she left her hand in his, enjoying the contact more than she was wiling to admit, even to herself. 'Perhaps I'm going to embarrass you tonight. You know I'm not at all commercial. I don't think I'm capable of making a good impression on a businessman.'

'You made a good impression on me.' Raul adjusted his long stride to match hers. 'And I'm a businessman.'

Her heart turned over at the unexpected compliment. 'You're lots of different things.'

'Desperate,' he said dryly, his smile full of wry self-mockery as he glanced at her. 'That's what I am at the moment, *cariño*. Thanks to you.'

Awareness exploded inside her. 'I thought we were supposed to be avoiding the topic of sex.'

'We were.' He let out a frustrated sigh. 'It's *your* fault.'

She tried to ignore the electrified atmosphere and changed the subject swiftly. 'So what do you want me to do this evening, seriously?'

'Try not to draw attention to yourself so that you don't distract me from the business in hand. This is a particularly tricky negotiation and I need to concentrate.' He took her hand in his and led her towards the main house just as a car purred into the courtyard.

'It's really that important to you? Any chance that you'll tell me why at some point?'

He didn't answer her question, and when she glanced towards him he was staring down the long driveway at an approaching car. Gone was the lazy, sexy smile that had made him so approachable. Now he just seemed cold and intimidating.

The car came to a halt in a cloud of dust and a man heaved himself awkwardly from the driver's seat, a sheen of sweat visible on his brow as he negotiated the heat and the demands of his own excessive body-weight. Faith guessed him to be in his fifties but it was obvious that he was holding on to his youth with grim determination. His shirt was open at the neck and strained over his thickened waist, his thinning hair artfully arranged to conceal the onset of baldness.

'Vásquez—I hear congratulations are due.'

'Pedro.' His hand outstretched and his tone cool, Raul strode forward and shook the man's hand and Faith watched while the other door opened and a woman slid elegantly out of the passenger seat.

Suddenly Faith understood why the man was so grimly determined not to be parted from his youth. The woman was stunning. She somehow managed to be both slender and curvaceous at the same time and the coal-black hair that hung straight over her bare shoulders shone like polished agate. Apparently undisturbed by the heat, she slowly removed the oversized sunglasses from her exquisite face to reveal almond-shaped eyes of surprising warmth. A friendly smile on her glossy mouth, she walked over to Faith, hands outstretched.

'So Raul finally took the plunge,' she said cheerfully, leaning forward and kissing Faith on both cheeks. Then she linked arms with her, as though they were firm friends, rather than total strangers. 'Half of Argentina is ready to kill you—the female half, of course. The male half are probably incredibly grateful. Finally they can sleep easy in their beds without feeling they need to lock up their wives. I'm Sofia.'

Confused by the other woman's direct approach and unsure how to respond, Faith glanced towards Raul but he was listening to something that Pedro was saying, his dark glossy head tilted because he was so much taller. Realising that he wasn't paying her any attention, Faith turned back to Sofia and froze.

The other woman was staring openly at Raul, a look of naked sexual appreciation in her eyes. Then she looked at Faith and grinned sheepishly. 'Oops, sorry. Caught red-handed.' She gave herself a mock smack on the wrist. 'Naughty me. But you have to admit that he *is* indecently handsome and I don't get to look at men like him very often. I'm sure you're used to women gazing at him. Being with Raul is a bit like owning a very rare and valuable painting— everyone wants to stare at it.'

Shocked and surprised by the hot spurt of jealousy that pumped through her veins, Faith struggled to stay polite. 'And your husband doesn't mind?'

'I can't imagine he'd be thrilled, but he has nothing to worry about. Raul and I were quite unsuited.'

Were?

For a moment Faith thought she had misheard, and then she looked into the other woman's eyes and her entire world shifted.

'You know him well?' *Why was she asking that question when she already knew the answer?*

'Pretty well.' Sofia looked at her. 'Oh dear. Me and my big mouth. Obviously the two of you haven't discussed his past. Very wise. If I was with Raul, I can't say I'd want to know about his past, either. One of the disadvantages of being with an *extremely* rich and handsome man is the knowledge that every other woman wants him too.'

'Sofia…' Raul's voice came from directly

behind them and Sofia turned, her eyes dancing with laughter.

'Darling—no need to use that tone. I'm just pleased you finally found someone willing to put up with your domineering, macho ways on a permanent basis. How are you? You're looking good, but there's nothing new in that.'

Before Raul could respond, Pedro approached. Apparently unaware of the byplay, he was mopping his brow. 'Shall we get out of the heat?'

'Of course. We'll have drinks on the terrace.'

Pinned to the spot by shock, Faith looked at Raul in disbelief.

That was it? *That was all he was going to say?*

Tact and sensitivity wasn't his strong suit and she, more than anyone, was well aware of that— but still she couldn't quite believe that he'd intentionally invited his ex-mistress to join them for dinner without at least warning her.

It must have been an unfortunate coincidence.

She desperately wanted to believe that he hadn't known the woman was with Pedro—that any minute now he was going to throw her off his property. Because the alternative to that was to acknowledge that once again her feelings had been bottom of his agenda.

'It's cooler on the terrace,' Raul said smoothly, nothing in his body language suggesting that he considered anything to be amiss.

Faith flinched as though he'd struck her.

So that was it, then.

Clearly he expected her to smile and chat to his ex, while he concentrated on his business deal.

No wonder he hadn't told her what was expected of her.

He'd obviously known that she would have been on the first plane out of Buenos Aires.

Raul strode across the courtyard, Pedro by his side, nothing in his manner betraying the slightest hint of awkwardness.

Deprived of the opportunity to claw his impossibly handsome face, Faith wanted to turn and stalk in the opposite direction, but she was unable to do that either because the other woman tightened her hold on her arm.

'We have a word in Spanish to describe someone like him,' Sofia murmured, her voice like rich honey. '*Guapisimo*. It means "indescribably handsome". I haven't been here for a while,' she confided, as they moved onto the sunny, vine-covered terrace where several staff were poised ready to serve drinks. 'You must show me what Raul has done. This place is the talk of the international polo-circuit.'

Faith didn't bother replying—she was too busy planning ways to kill Raul—but first she turned some serious anger onto herself.

You fool, she chided herself. *You stupid fool.*

He said he wanted the marriage to work and that was all it took for you to run back to him.

He'd hurt her so, so badly but had she learned her lesson? No, she'd come back for more.

Was he being deliberately cruel? Was he reminding her once again that she'd driven him into a marriage, when in fact that wasn't what he'd wanted?

Was he was telling her that marriage wasn't going to stop him living his life the way he wanted to live it?

Was that what was going on here?

A wave of dizziness washed over her and for a terrifying moment she thought she might faint in front of him yet again. Gritting her teeth with determination, she took several deep breaths and took a glass of champagne from one of Raul's staff. Deciding that it would be kill or cure, she drained it in several gulps.

Dimly aware of Raul's disapproving and

slightly startled gaze, she raised the empty glass in his direction. 'To us, darling. And to all those little things you do for me that show just how much you care.'

His eyes narrowed, but whether or not he would have responded to her subtle jibe she had no idea because Pedro dutifully lifted his glass.

'To the pair of you. May you have a long and happy union.'

Faith was deeply regretting the fact that she'd downed the champagne. Her head was swimming again, and now she wasn't sure of the cause.

'So what is it that you do, Faith?' Pedro was blunt and straightforward but Faith was spared the need to reply by his wife's intervention.

'She's married to Raul,' Sofia murmured. 'Which means her time is totally occupied in the pursuit of looking gorgeous.' Her gaze lingered speculatively on Faith's newly cropped hair and Faith flushed.

'I'm a vet. I specialise in horses. Raul has an interesting breeding programme so I chose to come here and work.' *And never left.* But she would now. Any moment. She was going to walk out of the door and not look back.

As soon as she could be sure that her legs would hold her.

'Breeding? Well if there's anyone who could use some advice in that area, then it's Raul.' Sofia laughed. 'Breeding is probably the only area of life in which he has absolutely no experience. I never could quite see him changing a nappy.'

Faith glanced at Raul and found him looking at her. 'Faith is exceptionally talented. Especially with the animals themselves.'

Did he even realise that she was upset?

Deciding that she wasn't going to inflate his ego still further by showing him how much his careless behaviour had upset her, Faith stood her ground.

Apparently unaware of the dangerous shift in the atmosphere, Pedro took a mouthful of his champagne. 'One of my stallions is misbehaving—kicking out his box, biting his groom—the product of an extremely difficult early life, I wouldn't be surprised. He's born vicious.'

'No horse is born vicious.' Faith's years of training made it impossible for her to stay silent. 'It's the way they've been treated that makes them that way. If he's vicious then he obviously feels he needs to defend himself from something.' Her eyes still held Raul's. 'All of us have the potential to be vicious if the provocation is sufficient.'

Raul's eyes narrowed but Pedro simply nodded, his mind clearly still on the problem of his horse.

'You could be right. To be honest, I have no idea what's in his past. My stud groom rescued him from somewhere or other. Thought he had potential. I'm not so sure. I think he needs to be taught who's boss.'

A bubble of laughter rose in Faith's throat. 'In my experience a display of macho domination rarely achieves the desired effect. I've always found that people respond better when you aim for a partnership of trust and respect.'

'People?' Pedro looked at her quizzically. 'I thought we were talking about horses.'

'Horses, people.' Faith shrugged. 'The principles are the same. The foundation of a good relationship is trust and respect.' She emphasised both words and Raul shot her a warning glance, which she interpreted as meaning: *be careful. This deal is important to me.*

And suddenly she wondered if he really did care about anything other than the acquisition of wealth.

Why else would he have chosen to flaunt his previous relationships in front of his wife?

Still apparently oblivious to the undercurrents swirling around them, Pedro drained his champagne. 'You're letting a woman dictate how your horses are handled, Vásquez?'

'I employ the best.'

Pedro frowned. 'I don't think I've ever met a female vet before.'

Faith took a sip of orange juice. 'Well, we're pretty much the same as the male variety, only we're usually a little smaller because our bodies don't have to make room for the ego.'

Sofia laughed with delight. 'I absolutely adore the English sense of humour.'

Pedro reached for a handkerchief and mopped his brow. 'I know it isn't considered politically correct to say so, but I still don't believe that a woman can do everything a man can do.'

'I completely agree.' Faith took another sip of her orange juice. 'No matter how hard I try I simply can't behave in a callous, insensitive fashion. Fortunately that major defect in my character hasn't affected my ability as a vet. Generally animals respond very well to a woman's touch.'

Finally alerted to the fact that the atmosphere wasn't all it should be, Pedro glanced at Raul who displayed a characteristic lack of concern.

'As you can see, my wife is as spirited as the

horses she loves so much. Faith is extremely well qualified.'

Pedro's eyebrows shot upwards. 'If she's that well qualified, why doesn't she have her own practice?'

'She met me,' Raul murmured. 'And I derailed her career.'

'Postponed,' Faith corrected him sharply. 'I can return to my career any time I choose to do so.'

Sofia smiled. 'So you fell in love.'

'Who wouldn't love Argentina?' Faith deliberately chose to misunderstand her. 'It's a fascinating and beautiful country. And the perfect place to practise equine medicine.'

'He's dangerous in the stable.' Pedro was back to the subject of his horse. 'We can't let him out, he'll create havoc.'

'But horses are herd animals,' Faith said. 'They like social contact. Especially the stallions. They are naturally dominant and assertive.'

'Sounds uncannily like Raul,' Sofia drawled. 'Dominant, assertive, a challenge to handle…'

Faith looked at her, startled, because actually the description she'd used *did* sound like Raul.

How many difficult stallions had she handled

who'd appeared to give no thought to the effect they had on those around them?

He probably hadn't invited his ex-mistress here with the express purpose of upsetting her. He'd invited her here because he was thoughtless. But did that really make his actions any more acceptable?

How in a million years could she ever be happy with a man this insensitive to her feelings?

Deep in thought, Pedro didn't appear to have heard his wife's comment. 'I might send him over to you, if that is within your realm of experience? Might be a bit much for you.'

Raul frowned. 'There's nothing Faith can't handle. She's very clever.'

'There's nothing clever about it,' Faith said. 'They just need patience and understanding.'

'Now I'm really confused.' A cheeky gleam in her eyes, Sofia laughed. 'Are we talking about Raul or the stallion? Clearly Faith has a special way with difficult men, since she dragged you to the altar.' Sofia slid her arm into Faith's again. 'And now, enough of this. Raul if you don't feed me soon I swear I shall join the horses in your yard. They're better cared for.'

CHAPTER NINE

THEY enjoyed a typical Argentine *asado*—a barbecue cooked over an open fire—and it was dark when Faith and Raul waved their guests off and walked back towards the Beach House.

Furious with him for hurting her and even more furious with herself for caring, Faith stalked ahead, her heels tapping on the path. She didn't trust herself to speak for fear of exploding and she wasn't sure whether she'd produce tears or anger.

'When you're angry, your neck seems longer,' Raul drawled from behind her and she straightened her shoulders and increased her pace. 'And that won't work, either, because my legs are longer than yours and I can walk faster.'

She turned then, like a cornered animal ready to fight. 'Do you really want to have this conversation out here? Think hard, Raul, because you probably won't want an audience for what I'm going to say.'

Apparently unconcerned, he lifted a bronzed hand to his throat and loosened the top button of his shirt. 'I thought we'd had enough conversation for one day.'

'If you want to avoid conversation, *don't* invite your ex-girlfriends to dinner without at least having the courtesy to warn me.'

Raul's eyes narrowed defensively. 'Given that you are the one wearing the wedding ring, you have absolutely no reason to be jealous.'

'It isn't about being jealous, it's about courtesy.' Faith kept her eyes on his, ignoring the dangerous shimmer in his eyes that warned her of the shift in his mood. 'Let's look at this another way—what would you have done if you discovered that I had invited an ex-boyfriend to dinner?'

'Flattened him,' Raul said in a cool tone. 'But that's entirely different.'

'It is *not* different. I have feelings, Raul. It would be nice if you would remember that.' Shaking so much she could hardly stand, she turned sharply and walked through the door of the Beach House. Dropping her bag as she walked, she went straight through to the bedroom and removed her earrings, dropping them on the bedside table.

'I don't understand your problem.' He stalked into the room like a very angry jungle-cat and she clamped her teeth onto her lower lip to stop herself from crying.

'I know you don't,' she whispered. 'And that *is* the problem, Raul. You don't seem to be able to stop yourself hurting me. You never think about *my* feelings and I promised myself that I wasn't going to allow you to do this to me again.' She kept her back to him, willing herself not to break down and sob.

'That is a totally unfair accusation,' he snarled, 'Given that it was precisely to protect your feelings that I didn't tell you.'

'So in other words, you knew I would be upset.'

She turned and then wished she hadn't because the physical impact of the man almost fused her brain. He was extravagantly, impossibly handsome, his features bold and masculine, his posture one of complete control.

Immediately on the defensive, his fabulous dark eyes narrowed to two dangerous slits. 'I thought you'd behave like a typical woman, and you've just proved me right.'

Faith inhaled sharply. 'She taunted me with your relationship. Waved it under my nose like a red flag. *We have a word for him in Spanish—* guapisimo.' She mimicked the other woman perfectly and then glared. 'Well let's see how *guapisimo* you are when I've blacked your eye, Raul.'

'You are behaving in a totally unreasonable fashion.'

'You think it's unreasonable of me to be upset?'

'Frankly? Yes. She's history.'

'She couldn't take her eyes off you!'

'That's her problem, not mine,' Raul replied instantly. 'And not yours, either.'

He didn't have a clue!

'Perhaps I am being silly but she knew a great deal about you,' she breathed. 'And I couldn't work out whether she was being friendly or nasty. But I had the distinct impression that she wished she was the one who was married to you.'

'She wouldn't have been able to handle me in a million years.' He yanked the tie from his throat with an impatient hand and Faith swallowed, transfixed by the hint of bronzed male skin and the tangle of dark hair at the base of his throat.

She wasn't sure *she* could handle him.

'She is very beautiful.'

'Don't do this to yourself,' he warned, dropping the tie and slowly undoing the buttons on his shirt. 'You're more intelligent than that, Faith. I never pretended not to have a past and you have no reason to be insecure.'

'Of course I have,' Faith said quietly. 'I know you didn't want this marriage.'

'Don't do that female thing of dissecting every single action,' he warned in a throaty voice. 'You'll just hurt yourself.'

'I just spent an evening with a woman who hammered home just how well she knows you. If I didn't have doubts about sustaining this marriage before, then I certainly have them now.'

'Sofia has *nothing* to do with our marriage.'

'You invited your ex-girlfriend into our home without telling me and expected me to be nice to her! That has *everything* to do with our marriage.'

They were circling each other like animals and the atmosphere in the room heated and sparked.

Raul watched her with raw frustration. 'Actually, I invited a business associate into our home in order to negotiate an important deal. Sofia just happens to be his wife. I didn't think that was important, given that she's my *ex*-girlfriend. What possible reason would there be for you to be so upset?'

'Because *I'm your wife!*'

'Precisely,' he drawled in a sardonic voice, his handsome face cold and unsympathetic. *'Cuenta his beneficios.'*

'What does that mean?'

'Count your blessings. *You're* the one wearing my ring. If anyone around here should be upset, it's Sofia, not you.'

Faith was so shocked by his unique interpretation of the facts, that for a moment she couldn't voice a response. 'You can't possibly mean that. Even you can't be *that* arrogant and insensitive.'

The air around them heated to a fierce blaze.

'Don't do this, Faith,' he warned softly, his voice as deadly as the expression in his eyes. *'Don't do this to us.'*

'I'm not the one doing it, Raul,' she spat, but she saw him step towards her and every muscle in her body quivered with tension. 'That's far enough.'

If he came close to her, *if he touched her…*

Terrified that he was going to do just that, she went to stalk past him but he moved so swiftly that she didn't stand a chance. And she knew deep down that she'd never had a chance. With merciless intent one hand locked around her wrist and the other came round her waist.

'No, Raul.' She squirmed and writhed, the silk of her dress sliding against the hard muscle of his thighs. 'Don't you *dare* touch me. After what you did tonight, you're never touching me again!' But they were just words and both of them knew it. The atmosphere was thick with what they were both feeling, and in many ways that made it worse because she so badly wanted to be able to walk away from this man. 'Let me go.'

'Why?' He brought his mouth close to hers and she turned her head to avoid the contact, her eyes closing as she felt the roughness of his jaw scrape the sensitive skin of her cheek. 'Why would I do that?'

'Because we're making each other miserable.'

'Only when we talk, *cariño*,' he murmured softly into her ear, his low masculine voice as sensuous as his touch. 'We hadn't touched each other for weeks and it's been driving both of us mad—'

'No, Raul, that isn't—' She broke off with a gasp as his mouth traced the line of her jaw. 'Don't do that—don't do that.'

But he wasn't listening. 'I haven't paid you enough attention.'

'That isn't what I was saying—' She moaned

as his mouth found the tiny pulse at the base of her throat. 'Raul, I'm asking you not to—'

'What? You're asking me not to do what?' His strong fingers slid around her cheek and with firm, relentless pressure he drew her lips back towards his. His mouth hovered a breath away from hers, but he didn't take the kiss. 'Why do you fight this?'

'Because I have to,' she whispered. 'For my sanity and my self-respect.' It was the last desperate plea of someone who was drowning and the words turned to a groan as his mouth finally brushed hers in a suggestive, sensuous kiss.

Flames erupted though her body with explosive force and she felt her insides turn to hot, molten lava.

'You don't want this?' His tone husky and full of dark, sexual promise, he lowered his head and lightly explored the edges of her mouth with his, the erotic slide of his tongue plunging her straight into a whirlpool of excitement. She was sucked downwards, spinning, in sexual free-fall. 'If you don't want to do this, then stop me,' he murmured, his mouth still against hers as he ruthlessly used every skill to drive her wild. 'Walk away, if that's what you want to do.'

Every single part of her was on fire, burning up in the heat of his seduction. 'How can I when you're holding me?'

His dangerously clever mouth curved into a sardonic smile. 'I let go of you five minutes ago, *cariño*. So why are you still pressed up against me?' He gave her less than five seconds for the truth of that statement to sink into her fevered brain and then he brought his mouth down on hers in a bruising, glorious kiss that sent both of them out of control.

This time there was no careful teasing or skilfully orchestrated seduction. There were no tentative touches of his tongue or sly brushes of his firm lips. Instead he claimed her mouth with his, driving out her protests with the force of his kiss.

And she responded because the way he kissed her demanded nothing less.

All the emotion and incredible tension that had been building over the past weeks exploded to the surface and they devoured each other hungrily as their bodies thundered with need.

His mouth didn't leave hers but his hands dropped to her shoulders and he tore ruthlessly through the fabric of her dress. It slithered to the floor of the bedroom and was instantly forgotten by both of them because his hand was on her breast and Faith gave an agonised moan and closed her eyes.

Her head was filled with a kaleidoscope of light, and as his fingers grazed the sensitised peaks of her breasts, sharp arrows of desire shot through her body straight to the very heart of her. She leaned into him, pressing herself against his throbbing, thickened shaft, her response to him every bit as animal and basic as his was to hers.

They had no control. None. And it had always been this way with them.

'Now,' Faith sobbed. 'Now—' And she tore impatiently at his shirt, drew her nails through the dark hair that covered his chest and then moved her hand lower to cover him. His responsive groan echoed her own desperation and when he lifted her, she slipped both arms round his neck because to let him go now would have been unthinkable.

Neither of them was thinking, each of them just responding to a sensual hunger so basic that it bordered on the shocking.

She wanted to touch and taste and he obviously felt the same way because his hand went between her legs and she cried out and arched against him in instant response. When he drew a skilled finger over her silken warmth, she gave a shiver of delicious pleasure, the anticipation exploding inside her.

Somehow she was on her back on the bed and he was above her—bronzed, virile and very much in control. When his mouth found her breast she sobbed with pleasure and when his fingers slid deep, she raked her nails over the hard muscle of his shoulders because his touch was so unerringly skilled and confident that she could do nothing else.

The room was dark except for a shaft of moonlight that sent a spotlight across the floor and she opened her eyes and looked straight into his. Dark locked with green for a fiery, breathless moment and she just feasted on him, savouring the hard, packed muscle of his shoulders and chest and the perfect lines of his bone structure. He was hot, hard, handsome and *hers*—all arrogant, dominant male, the weight of his powerful body pinning her into a position of total submission.

'Mine,' he growled possessively, his hand in the silken curls that guarded the most private part of her. 'You are mine—'

'Yes—' She didn't want to be anyone else's

ever and just to be sure that he knew that she slid her leg over his thigh in a blatant invitation that drew a groan from him.

'Wait.' His breathing erratic, he swore softly in Spanish. There was a brief pause and then he surged into her with all the force of his passion, the power of his silken invasion driving her breath from her body because he was big.

Hard and powerful, he filled her completely and for a moment she struggled to breathe, completely overwhelmed by the feel of him deep inside her. Engulfed by excitement that terrified her in its intensity, she stared up at him in the semi-darkness, completely transported by the exquisite pleasure that their bodies created together. There was nothing but the two of them, their bodies locked in one glorious explosion of excitement as he drove into her with ravenous, fiery intensity. His hand was locked in her hair, her nails were in his shoulders and she urged him on with the thrust of her hips, her legs spread for him, her back pressed against the bed.

'Raul—' She groaned his name and he slid an arm under her hips, strong, virile and demanding as he lifted her into each surging thrust of his powerful body.

It was wild, uninhibited and out of control and when she shot into her first orgasm she took him with her, his body erupting with potent force as her inner muscles tightened around him. Mouths clashed, hearts raced, breathing quickened as every one of their senses was swamped by incredible sensation and they drove each other through wave after wave of pulsing ecstasy. Bodies slick and hot, they kissed their way through the whole incredible experience until the explosion was reduced to flickering, fluttering aftershocks.

Lying on the tangled sheets, weakened by pleasure, Faith wrapped her arms around him tightly and waited for her heartbeat to slow. She was so dazed after her climax that when he slid down her body and deliberately parted her thighs, she was unable to do more than whimper a faint protest.

'I love your body,' he murmured, his lips trailing a path that started at her knee and slowly traced the length of her thigh. 'Do you know how much I love your body? Because if you don't then I'm about to show you...'

Her brain and body still pulsing in the aftermath of her last orgasm, Faith tried to squirm away from him, too weakened to even consider another sensual onslaught.

'No, Raul,' she choked. 'I don't think I can—'

'Then I'll prove you wrong,' he said huskily, guiding her thighs apart with single-minded focus and complete disregard for any modesty on her part. He held her there for a moment, surveying the tangle of bright golden curls with a hungry, sexual gaze that made her squirm self-consciously.

'Don't.'

'I'm admiring.' His mouth curved into a slow, teasing smile. 'How can you be shy? On the surface you can be very English and proper.' He stroked a strong confident finger along the most intimate part of her and she curled her fingers into the sheets because he knew exactly what he was doing, his gentle touch impossibly, agonisingly accurate.

'Raul—?'

'But *below* the surface—' his finger slid deep inside her '—you are wild. All bubbling passion. All mine.' And to prove that point, he lowered his head and slid his tongue over the delicate bud of her womanhood and she cried out in shock because her whole body reacted so dramatically to his touch.

She was consumed by arousal, acutely conscious of every move he made; of the restless flick of his tongue, the flex of muscle as he supported himself on his arms, the roughness of his jaw against the smooth skin of her inner thigh—and it was so agonisingly perfect and he was so skilled that she shot into another climax that he caught with his mouth and fingers.

He slid up her body, fastened his mouth to hers and kissed her deeply, and then he shifted slightly and turned her over. For a moment Faith just lay on her front, her eyes closed, her body still quivering from the touch of his mouth. Then she felt him move and gasped as his hard fingers captured her hips and lifted her onto her knees.

'Raul—'

'I *love* it this way,' he groaned and before she could wriggle away or protest that she just wasn't ready for more, *that she just couldn't do this again*, he sank into her with a decisive thrust.

Her trembling, sensitised body clamped around his in ecstatic pleasure, apparently ignoring her brain, which was telling her that she just couldn't be doing this again.

He surged deep into her slick heat and it felt so mind-blowingly good that she cried out in shock. In this position he controlled her utterly, his hands holding her bottom, the roughness of the hair on his thighs brushing against her soft flesh. The ache inside her grew and grew with each purposeful thrust of his body and the slow ripples of pleasure spread and built to a crescendo until she was caught in a vortex of excitement so intense that she lost touch with reality.

She was on fire, her senses stormed by an attack of almost excruciating pleasure, her climax so intense that she barely registered the rhythmic thrusts that signalled his own release. For a moment there was nothing but pure, blind ecstasy, a shower of erotic sensations that left her in a state of numb shock and speechless disbelief.

Boneless and exhausted, Faith flopped forwards onto the bed in a weakened, quivering state and Raul sprawled next to her, his lean, powerful body suddenly relaxed, the smile on his face clearly reflecting his belief in his own sexual supremacy.

For a moment Faith just lay there, too shattered to speak. Part of her was afraid to move or draw attention to herself in any way in case he just hauled her against him and tried yet another position. And another part of her—a wicked, wanton part of her that she didn't understand—wanted him to do just that because he was so incredibly gifted and she couldn't get enough of him.

Acknowledging that fact made her turn her face into the sheets with a groan of disbelief and mortification. No matter how she liked to pride herself on her brain, she was a complete pushover when it came to this man.

He only had to touch her and she was his. Every time. Every way. Whenever he wanted.

And just what would her pathetic display of female submission have done to his already over-inflated ego?

Raul already thought he was the best and hadn't she just gone right ahead and proved it?

She raised herself on her elbow but before she could speak or do anything, he rolled her onto her back and flattened her to the bed again, his gaze surprisingly gentle as he studied her from beneath thick, dark lashes.

That long, slumberous look softened everything inside her and her stomach and heart performed a series of acrobatics as she stared up at him.

He *cared*, she knew he did and her own gaze softened in response as she waited for him to say something affectionate. After what they'd shared, how could he fail to?

He stroked her flushed cheek with gentle fingers and lowered his head to kiss her gently on the mouth.

'*Now* talk to me about feeling insecure,' he breathed and then rose from the bed in a fluid movement and strode into the bathroom with long, confident strides.

Faith stared up at the ceiling in stunned, silent disbelief.

That was why he'd made love to her over and over again?

To try and prove that she had no reason to be jealous?

Feeling numb inside, she slid off the bed and followed him on shaking legs into the bathroom.

'Insecure?' She croaked the word from the doorway. 'That was why you made love to me? Not because you love me or wanted me, but just to prove a point?'

His strong, muscular body already under the shower, he gave a shrug of his shoulders. 'After the last few hours it should be obvious that I'm not thinking of any woman other than you.'

Faith swallowed. 'I wanted you to think about my feelings. A conversation would have done the trick.'

'I've always been more of a practical kind of guy,' he drawled, tilting his head back so that the water cascaded over his glossy dark hair and bronzed shoulders. 'And that is a ridiculous accusation because I have been thinking of nothing *but* your feelings for the past few hours, *cariño*.' Wiping the water from his eyes, he threw her a sexy, suggestive smile.

'Not those sorts of feelings!' This was the wrong place to have this talk, Faith realised numbly. He was gloriously, unashamedly naked, his aggressively masculine body proudly on display in front of her and she just couldn't concentrate because she was agonisingly aware of his broad, powerful shoulders, the burst of dark body hair that shadowed the centre of his chest and the impressive contours of his manhood.

Averting her eyes, she concentrated her attention on the neat pile of towels. 'Tell me something,' she asked shakily. 'Why is it that you think sex solves everything?'

Without answering her question, he stemmed the flow of the water and stepped out of the shower, completely unselfconscious. 'Towel, please?'

She handed him a towel and too late realised her mistake because he closed his fingers around her wrist and hauled her hard against his damp, naked body. 'You want to know why it is that I think sex solves everything?' His mouth hovered above hers and his damp, heated skin brushed her quivering flesh. 'Before, we were arguing and you were angry with me. You were spitting like an angry cat and now you no longer want to spit and you are no longer angry—so you see sex *does* solve problems.' Having driven home his point, he released her and raked wet spears of hair from his eyes with strong, confident fingers while Faith stared at him helplessly.

'I feel more like your mistress than your wife.'

Raul shot her a meaningful look. 'Considering the effect that marriage can have on a couple's sex life, you should be relieved about that.'

'You think you're such a genius in bed, don't you?'

'No.' He hooked the towel round his waist and gave her a slow, dangerous smile. '*You* are the one who makes me think I am a genius in bed. You melt, you sob.' He shrugged. 'You like what I do to you, *cariño*.'

Knowing that it was true, her cheeks coloured. 'I promised myself I wasn't going to let you hurt me again, Raul.'

He frowned. 'I made sure you were protected.'

'I didn't mean that,' she muttered and his eyes narrowed.

'So what then? I was too rough?'

'No!' She was silent for a moment, impossibly aware of his searching gaze. 'It doesn't matter.'

'*Sí*, it matters. If it brings that look into your eyes after we have made love, then it matters.' With an impatient sigh, he took her face in his hands and stroked his thumbs over her cheeks. 'All right, if you want to talk, we will talk. Go on. I'm listening.'

'That isn't enough! You have to do some of the talking, too. This chemistry between us is amazing, we make love and it's like nothing I've ever felt before.' It was difficult for her to be so painfully honest because she was making herself vulnerable and he was so completely *in*vulnerable. 'When we're together like this I feel so close to you but when it's over I realise that I'm not close at all. It's just physical. I don't *know* you at all. We don't talk. Even tonight we didn't talk because the moment I raised a problem, you just turned to sex. I really do feel more like your mistress than your wife.'

'A woman thinks she wants a man to be honest with her but what she is *really* saying is that she wants that man to tell her what she wants to hear.' His tone was cool. 'I'm not like that. I don't lie.'

'All right, fine, don't lie. *But I need you to think about my feelings!'*

He released her and stepped away. 'This business with Pedro is concluded. You won't have to see Sofia again.'

'It isn't just about Sofia. She's just a symptom of what's wrong with our relationship—the fact that we don't *talk*. When we have a problem, I want us to talk about it. I don't just want you to throw me on the bed and have sex with me! I want to *know* you, Raul. And if the truth about how you feel is painful to hear, so be it. At least it's the truth. I want to know you and I want you to know me.'

His dark eyes were shuttered and she almost felt his emotional retreat.

'That is why women have female friends, so that they can chew over issues that are entirely irrelevant to men.' Raul released her and stepped away, his handsome face cold. 'I just gave you a whole lot of messages, all of them positive. If you choose not to read them, then it's up to you.' He strode back into the bedroom leaving her staring after him in exasperation.

Exhausted after her sexual marathon with Raul, Faith slept late and woke to find Raul gone.

Deciding that she needed a distraction, she dressed quickly and walked over to the stables.

As usual they were a hive of activity and Eduardo greeted her with his usual warmth. 'It is good to see you back. Raul is on the polo field, working off his energy with some of the guests.'

Faith spent a few minutes with her favourite horses and then walked towards the nearest polo field where a game was being played.

People came from all over the world to play polo on Raul's *estancia* but only rarely were they afforded the privilege of playing with the boss himself—but today, it seemed, was one of those prized occasions.

Raul thundered down the field with such an astonishing burst of acceleration that the watching crowd of guests and grooms gave a collective gasp. He rode his pony alongside his opponent's mount, moving him away from the ball so that he could take possession.

'And that's how it's done,' murmured one of the grooms who was watching. 'Just glorious.'

The ponies were drenched in sweat and above them the sun blazed in a perfectly blue sky.

Where did he find the stamina? Faith wondered, watching Raul demonstrate a move to one of the guests and then drive his horse down the field after the ball. He'd had virtually no sleep and yet he was as energetic as ever.

The temperature rocketed and dust flew from the ground as the ponies stampeded over the grass.

Faith watched him, thinking about the parallel Sofia had drawn between Raul and a stallion.

Even the most difficult stallion could be tamed.

But she hadn't tamed Raul, had she?

She'd trapped him. Not intentionally, but if she'd known how he'd felt she never would have gone ahead with the wedding, no matter how much she'd loved him. But the truth was that she'd loved him so much and she'd thought their relationship so perfect, that she hadn't even questioned his proposal. To her it had been a natural progression.

And he hadn't given her the chance to question it.

It was only now, looking back on it, that she

realised that from that point until the day of their wedding, he'd been running.

In the middle of delicate negotiations with some company in the Far East, he'd flown to Japan for two weeks and then on to New York.

He hadn't come home and at the time she hadn't thought it particularly odd. Raul set himself a punishing work schedule and his absence hadn't seemed particularly strange. *Until now.*

Faith watched as the horses came off the field and the grooms sprang into action. She'd been so wrapped up in her own emotions she hadn't really thought about his. When he'd immediately proposed marriage, she'd assumed everything was all right.

Naïvely thinking that their love had been sufficient for him to make him rethink his views on marriage, she'd gone ahead without questioning how he really felt.

Arrogance? She'd accused him of arrogance but she'd been the one with arrogance, hadn't she? She'd assumed that she was different from all the other women he'd ever been with. She'd thought that was why he'd been so eager to marry her.

Raul rode over to her and vaulted from his horse. 'You're awake.'

A groom took the horse from him and he walked with her back towards the Beach House. 'You're very quiet. Sofia again?'

'No.' Her voice was small because she was feeling completely and utterly tormented with guilt and Raul gave a driven sigh.

'I have no feelings for her whatsoever. I thought I'd made that clear.'

'Actually I'm not thinking about Sofia,' Faith muttered. 'I'm thinking about us. Our marriage. The baby.' She felt his immediate withdrawal and grabbed his hand in a desperate little movement, as if holding on to him physically might prevent his emotional retreat. 'Don't back off. I *know* this is difficult but will you at least talk?' She watched him, recognising all the signs as he placed himself well and truly on the defensive.

His eyes were hard as diamonds, his thin mouth an uncompromising line in his handsome face. Every muscle in his powerful frame vibrated with tension and his body language screamed 'keep off'. 'I *know* how upset you are about losing the baby. I fail to see what talking achieves unless you simply want to make me feel more guilty.' His raw tone stunned her.

'I—I'm not trying to make you feel guilty.' She shook her head. 'Why would you think that?'

He inhaled deeply and something flickered in the depths of his eyes. 'I suppose because I *do* feel guilty,' he confessed in a husky voice. 'You lost that baby because of me.'

'No—'

'I upset you—'

'*After* I lost the baby,' she said gently. 'And even if it had been before, you wouldn't have been the cause.' She swallowed and gave a painful smile. 'It wasn't anyone's fault, Raul. I think it's normal to feel like that, but it wasn't anyone's fault. Miscarriage is horribly common. A doctor in the hospital told me that—' She broke off for a moment, a rush of emotion catching her by surprise. 'He told me that some babies just don't stick and that is nature's way of saying that something isn't quite right.' Her hand was still on his arm and she felt the flex of muscle under her fingers.

'Fine.' His voice was as tense as his body. 'Good.'

'That wasn't what I wanted to say,' she mumbled quietly. 'I wanted to say that I'm sorry.'

He stilled, and a faint flush spread across his cheekbones, highlighting his striking features. 'So you admit that you became pregnant on purpose?'

'No!' Horrified by his interpretation of her apology, she stared at him. 'No. It was an accident.'

'Then why *are* you saying sorry?'

'Because I never once saw it from your point of view. And I've only just realised that,' Faith admitted wearily. 'I discovered I was pregnant and I was a bit nervous but when you immediately proposed, I assumed you were all right with it. I—I wasn't really thinking. I should have questioned you more closely. There was no way I would have married you if you had doubts.'

He was cold and uncommunicative. 'I didn't have doubts.'

'You didn't want to get married!'

'Once you told me you were pregnant, there was never a choice.'

'So you did the decent thing.' Admitting that was so hard and Faith gave a painful smile and let go of his arm. 'I thought you were marrying me because we had a good relationship,' she admitted. 'Silly me, hmm?' She tried to keep her tone light but the pain cracked her voice and she heard him inhale sharply.

'We *did* have a good relationship,' he snapped impatiently. 'We still do.'

'In the bedroom,' she said dryly and he frowned.

'That isn't true. We talk. You're a very intelligent woman and you have an opinion on everything.'

'We didn't talk about feelings,' Faith muttered. 'And especially we didn't talk about *your* feelings that I was pregnant. So I'm apologising for that. I'm sorry if this marriage wasn't what you wanted and I'm sorry I didn't stop you doing the decent thing.'

'*Nothing* you said or did would have stopped me marrying you,' Raul delivered in a forceful tone. 'So you can tick that problem off your list of things to talk about.'

'Maybe not when I was pregnant, but if I hadn't been pregnant or if I had told you I'd lost the baby before the wedding—' She broke off and he cursed softly, his dark eyes glinting with naked exasperation.

'Last night we were happy! Now you're upset and for no reason! This is why I don't like talking endlessly about issues that can't be changed.'

'Was it Sofia?' The question burst from her and she put a hand on his arm. 'Something must have made you feel this way. Was she the reason that you never wanted marriage or children? *Did she hurt you?*'

He shut down like a nuclear reactor in an emergency. Nothing was going to escape.

'We're married, Faith,' he said coldly. 'Leave it at that.'

And he turned and walked into the Beach House, the set of his shoulders warning her not to follow.

CHAPTER TEN

FAITH curled up on one of the white sofas in the Beach House, horribly conscious of Raul's absence and furious with herself for her lack of tact.

Why had she pushed him?

After their conversation—*the conversation that she'd forced*—he'd changed into a sleek dark suit, apparently cut to display every single one of his assets, and announced that he had business in Buenos Aires.

And she hadn't seen him since. Now she deeply regretted having brought the subject up. She should never have asked him why he didn't want babies and marriage and most particularly she should not have mentioned Sofia's name.

Wishing desperately that she could wind the clock back, Faith took a sip of water.

At some stage Maria had brought her some lunch, but she didn't feel like eating. Her stomach was churning and she felt horribly sick but she knew it was just nerves.

She was totally on edge and unable to relax. She'd tried to understand him and in the process she'd driven him away and now she didn't know how to solve the new problem she'd created. He was very upset, she knew that much. When Raul was cornered, he fought and when he couldn't fight, he retreated.

It reminded her of the day she'd told him about the baby. He'd immediately proposed, bought her a ring and then proceeded to absent himself on business. At the time she'd just assumed that was normal for him—after all he was a staggeringly successful billionaire with a corporation to run—but now she knew him better she could see that he'd been doing an entirely different sort of running. The sort that left a problem far behind.

And she wasn't much better, was she?

Hadn't she done exactly the same on their wedding day? True, he'd made a grossly insensitive remark but she wished now that she'd stood her ground and forced him to talk about it.

Yes, she'd been devastated about the baby but running hadn't helped.

They were both as bad as each other.

Except that she wasn't running any more. Nor was she going to try and push him to talk to her.

She was handling him all wrong, she could see that now. The more she pushed, the more he resisted. Somehow she needed to persuade him to come to her.

She stared at the food on her plate, deep in thought, her mind once again drifting back to the comment Sofia had made about Raul being like a difficult stallion. In a way she was right. There were similarities. Raul was aggressively masculine, assertive and dominant. And the way to handle that sort of personality was with gentleness and patience. There was no way she was going to force a man like Raul to tell her anything he didn't want to.

She had to earn his trust.

He hated talking about emotions, so she'd stop doing that.

She'd stop dwelling on the past and concentrate on the present—on being happy together. Even *he* had agreed that they'd been happy before she'd become pregnant. All she needed to do was try and recapture that. And as for what was going to happen in the long term—well, she wasn't even going to think about that now.

The sight of the food making her feel ill, she rose to her feet and wandered down to the beach with a book but she couldn't concentrate on that either, so she went to the stables instead, and worked alongside the grooms for the afternoon.

Being with the horses calmed her slightly but still she couldn't stop thinking about Raul and kept one eye on the drive, desperately hoping to hear the throaty roar of his car or the sound of the helicopter which would have announced his return.

Eventually she gave up watching and returned to the Beach House for a shower.

Still he didn't appear and she picked up the phone, intending to call him, and then put it down again instantly, afraid of looking needy— afraid that in his current mood he'd think she was hassling him.

Where was he?

Had she driven him away for good this time?

Exhausted and miserable, she lay down on the bed and turned out the light. What was the point in waiting up for him when he so clearly didn't want her company?

Having spent the day trying to work off his dangerous mood, Raul waited until dark to return to the Beach House, assuming that Faith would be asleep and he'd avoid another bout of female confrontation.

He spoke five languages fluently but never, ever would he understand women.

First she'd been angry with him and now she seemed to think he might need to talk about his feelings.

With an impatient frown, he threw his jacket down on the chair and poured himself a large drink.

Why was it that women thought that spilling their guts was a good thing?

As far as he was concerned it was a pointless exercise, designed to make everyone feel a thousand times worse. In his opinion, the secret of success lay in the ability to stifle and suppress any emotions that threatened one's equilibrium.

And thanks to Faith's persistent probing, his emotions were definitely threatening. She'd opened parts of his mind that he'd kept safely sealed for years.

His hand tightening around the glass, he swallowed the drink in one mouthful, ruthlessly pushing back against the thoughts that were closing in on him, cursing Faith for her desire to know him better.

She didn't want to know *that* part of him, he thought grimly, depositing the empty glass on the table.

Intentionally or not, she was edging him closer to something that he'd avoided for his entire adult life. It loomed in front of him, a dark, deadly swarm of dirty, foul emotions from his past.

Suddenly his phone rang, cutting through the silence, and he gave a soft curse and reached for it, afraid that the sound would wake her.

'It's me.' She stood in the doorway of the bedroom, her voice soft with sleep, the phone in her hand. 'I'm the one ringing you.'

'What for?' Bracing himself for more confrontation, Raul felt every muscle in his body tense to snapping point. 'Why are you ringing me at three in the morning?'

'Because I was worried.'

He scanned her in a single sweep of his gaze. Her feet were bare, her cheeks were flushed from sleep and she wore a tiny, flimsy sheath of silk, apparently designed with the express intention of driving a man out of his mind.

Raul instantly forgot to be angry. In fact his mind emptied itself of everything except thoughts of sex. His body responded with electrifying force, his groin sending urgent signals to his fevered brain. In the grip of an arousal that bordered on the painful, he eyed the sofa.

Hot and fast. Right here. Right now.

On the verge of grabbing her and spreading her flat, he caught the look in her green eyes and saw something that stopped him.

Concern.

She really had been worried about him.

Trying to remember the last time that anyone had worried about him, Raul stifled his instinctive desire to flatten her underneath him, sensing with an unusual degree of insight that this would not be a good move.

On the other hand, not flattening her underneath him didn't seem like a good move either.

'Are you all right? You're so, *so* tense. I can feel it from here.' She was staring anxiously at his face and Raul realised that she had absolutely no idea that she was responsible for the rocketing levels of his tension.

Exasperated with himself for not being able to control himself around her, he scanned his options swiftly.

'I need air,' he ground out, turning and striding out onto the beach in the hope that fresh air and distance might succeed where logic and will power had failed.

What was the matter with him?

Since when had his mind focused on nothing but sex?

He'd always had a high sex-drive, yes, but sex had never before intruded on his every waking moment until the day he'd first met Faith.

He inhaled deeply, searching for some semblance of the control on which he'd always prided himself.

Faced with nothing but the dark expanse of the ocean, the nagging throb in his body eased slightly and some of the tension left his shoulders. But his respite was short lived because he suddenly felt her arms slide around his waist. She leaned her head against his back in an affectionate gesture that took him by surprise.

'I love you.' She spoke the words softly but he heard them nonetheless and her honest declaration knocked the last of the breath from his lungs.

He felt at a loss and he *never* felt like that and when she walked round to stand in front of him, he braced himself for yet another serious disturbance to his emotional well-being.

But she didn't say a word.

Instead she lifted her hands and slowly undid the buttons on his shirt and slid her hands over his chest. Her fingers were warm and gentle and he sucked in a breath as she pushed the shirt from his shoulders. Then she touched her mouth to his flesh and the arousal he'd been fighting returned with twice the intensity.

Driven by the throbbing ache low in his body, Raul followed his instincts and slid his fingers into her hair, holding her still for his kiss. Passion exploded between them and his mouth devoured hers with explicit, erotic intensity. He felt her slender frame quivering against his, her uninhibited response sending his own levels of arousal soaring into the stratosphere.

But before he could follow his instincts and lower her onto the sand, she eased away from his grip and slid her hands over his chest.

'You're an incredible kisser.'

More than happy to demonstrate the full breadth of his skills, Raul reached for her again, but she evaded his grasp and pressed her mouth against his chest, her mouth slowly tracing the line of his body hair.

Then she dropped to her knees in the sand.

Her blonde hair was bright in the moonlight

and her green eyes sparkled like jewels as she threw him a look that blew the circuits in his mind. She was pure, lethal seductress and while Raul was still recovering from the shock of that look, she'd apparently finished the task of undressing him because he suddenly discovered that he was naked.

Accustomed to always being the aggressor when it came to sex, Raul's mind was still dragging far behind his body when he felt the scrape of her nails on his thighs and the warm flick of her tongue.

He uttered an oath and her response was to slide her mouth closer to his potent masculine arousal.

'*Don't* talk,' she ordered and Raul was more than happy to comply with that particular request because he no longer had the ability to string a sentence together. The subtle brush of her fingers against his bare flesh was so shockingly good that his abdomen clenched in violent anticipation. His body pulsed and throbbed but instead of doing what he ached for her to do, she teased him, as he had teased her so many times before, with lips, tongue and fingers, seducing and exciting until every bit of his body was pumped up and hard with arousal.

Just when he thought he was going to explode, she took him in her mouth and an earthy groan of disbelief tore from his throat.

His mind went totally blank and his entire world centred on that one, throbbing part of him. Nothing existed for him except the raging, burning heat in his loins and the incredible, unbelievable sensations created by her warm, damp, knowing mouth. That part of him was so shockingly sensitised that he was hyper-aware of every tiny movement she made—the flick of her tongue, the warmth of her breath, the brush of her fingers—and then it all merged and he felt his self-control splinter and crack as he was hurled headlong into the most all-consuming, violent, incredible climax of his life.

Completely unaware of time, Raul stood with his eyes tightly shut and his jaw clenched, waiting for his body and brain to return from that place of blind, sexual ecstasy.

Finally he opened his eyes and found himself staring straight into hers.

He opened his mouth, closed it again and then gave up on speech because this was one occasion when actions would definitely speak louder than words.

He lifted her and tumbled her gently down on

the sand, his body covering hers in a decisive, possessive movement but immediately she pushed at his chest.

'I want you on your back,' she breathed. 'I haven't finished.'

Raul rolled away from her immediately, too dazed even to question her. Part of him thought it only fair to warn her that he doubted his capability for more after what he'd just experienced, but already she was straddling him lightly, the smile on her lips pure temptress.

'Are you feeling OK, Raul?'

He was about to attempt some sort of response when she lowered herself onto his throbbing shaft and he discovered with electrifying force that his need for this woman knew no limitations.

She moved her hips slowly and skilfully and his hands closed on the curve of her bottom in an instinctive masculine need to increase the pace.

'No.' She leaned forward and teased his mouth with hers, the new angle of her body creating a wicked, delicious friction that drew another groan from deep within him.

He was on fire again, his entire body pumped up and primed to thrust but she didn't let him. Instead she teased him relentlessly, lowering her body and taking him deep and then staying perfectly still for just long enough for the desperate urgency in his loins to make a partial retreat.

Again and again she prolonged the agony until his body was screaming for completion and her eyes were glittering with her own excitement.

Driven past the point of control, Raul gripped her hips, positioned her as he wanted her and drove into her quivering, shivering, pliant body with an uninhibited wildness that bordered on the shocking. He felt her inner muscles grip him violently and for a moment they were both suspended in the grip of fierce, unbelievable pleasure.

Then she collapsed against him and he closed his arms around her, feeling the softness of her hair brushing against his jaw.

He was the first to break the silence. 'You've never done that before.'

'You've never given me a chance,' she said huskily. 'You just take the initiative every single time. I used to think I was quite a strong woman, and then I met you.'

'That's just because I can't look at you and not want to be inside you,' he groaned, his impossibly frank confession drawing a soft laugh from her.

'You're very dominating, do you know that?'

'Never again,' Raul vowed, stroking her soft hair with a reverential hand. 'It was amazing. *You* were amazing. From now on I'll just lie there and let you do all the work. I'll be passive.'

'Passive?' She lifted her head and her eyes sparkled into his. 'You couldn't be passive if you tried. You and passive are like oil and water, you just don't mix.'

'So why did you choose tonight?'

Her smile faded and there was a sudden shyness in her eyes. 'We had a problem. I didn't know how to get through to you.'

'I thought you said that sex doesn't solve problems.'

'It's always worked for you,' she muttered. 'I thought it was worth a try.'

'It worked.' He gave a groan and cupped her face in his hands, drawing her mouth to his. '*Dios mío*, it definitely worked. Any time you want to be dominating again, just go ahead.'

Faith woke to find Raul sprawled in a chair, a brooding expression on his handsome face as he watched her yawn and stretch.

'It's lunchtime,' he informed her smoothly and her eyes widened in surprise.

'It can't possibly be that late!'

'You just crashed out and you haven't moved since.' His eyes scanned her features with disturbing intensity. 'You are as pale as marble. I am going to ask the doctor to see you.'

'No.' She sat up and rubbed her eyes, embarrassed that she'd just slept for so long. 'There's no need. I'm fine, really. I was just tired. The last few weeks have been stressful.' The moment the words left her mouth she regretted them because she felt the immediate increase in his tension.

'I know, and since this is clearly the time for apologies, I'm willing to accept that some of this is my fault.'

Rendered speechless by that uncharacteristic declaration, Faith stared at him and he frowned.

'Don't look at me like that. Believe it or not, I am capable of apology when the need arises.' His eyes darkened and he looked at her for a moment and a faint smile of self-mockery touched his firm mouth. 'It's just that the need doesn't usually arise.'

She gave a wobbly smile. 'You don't have to apologise. I can see now why you were so upset.'

'You are very forgiving, but I shouldn't have made that comment at the wedding,' he breathed. 'It was insensitive of me and in a way I can understand why you ran away. I gave you no reason to believe our relationship could work, but it can, *cariño*. I *do* care about your feelings and just to prove that I've arranged a very special trip for us.'

'You have?' She sensed the change in him but didn't understand it. *Was this to do with last night?* Whatever had caused it, she wasn't about to question it and risk ruining it in any way.

'You missed out on a honeymoon,' he drawled softly. 'So that's what I've arranged. I'm very aware that when you first came to Argentina you planned to travel around the country and meeting me stopped all that.'

Faith curled up on the bed, butterflies in her stomach as she watched him. He was *so* confident and handsome, so utterly sure of himself, how could any woman ever resist him? Looking at him now, she wasn't surprised that she'd made the decision that she had. 'I don't regret anything, Raul.'

'I'm taking you somewhere really special. You deserve it.'

'When will we go?'

'How soon can you dress?' Raul's glance was faintly mocking. 'My pilot is waiting for us.'

Faith gasped and slipped out of bed. 'Right now?'

'Of course. Why not?'

His response made her smile. With Raul everything had to be right now. His capacity for waiting for anything was severely limited. 'I can be dressed in two minutes,' she assured him, reaching into her wardrobe for something comfortable to wear. 'But I need to pack.'

'That's all been dealt with.' Raul flipped his phone out of his pocket and spoke briefly to his pilot. 'Just bring yourself.'

Faith selected a pair of shoes from the dozens of pairs he'd given her. 'But where exactly are we going?'

'We're going to play tourist.' Taking her hand in a firm grasp, he led her out of the Beach House towards the helipad that was positioned just behind the polo fields.

'But everything will be booked up at this short notice.'

Urging her into the helicopter that bore the logo of his company, he greeted that comment with a glance of shimmering amusement. 'Then my staff will just have to *un*book it.'

And no doubt some ordinary mortal was about

to be booted out of the room they'd booked months ago, Faith thought weakly as she sank into her seat and ruefully contemplated the benefits of being in love with a sexy billionaire. His money wasn't what had attracted her, but she was intelligent enough to recognise that the aspects of his character that she found so compelling were the same qualities that drove his success. His astonishingly quick brain, his confidence, his insight and his hard, ruthless ability to outsmart the competition—all those things made him the man he was.

And she loved him.

Her heart skipped and danced as he sprawled in the seat next to her and took her hand in his.

'My private jet is waiting for us at the airport.' He stretched out his legs. 'Get some rest, *cariño*, you're going to need it.'

He took her to Iguazú Falls, on the border with Brazil, and she gazed in disbelief at the hundreds of cascades that stretched before her in a horseshoe shape.

'I've only ever seen one waterfall at a time before,' she said faintly and Raul settled himself behind her and pulled her against his hard body.

'There are about two hundred and seventy-five

different cascades,' he murmured in her ear. 'We share the falls with Brazil but two thirds are on the Argentine side.'

She could hear the pride in his voice and Faith laughed and twisted round so that she could look at him. 'You always have to be the biggest and the best, don't you?'

His answer was to kiss her and it was another few minutes before she was able to turn her attention back to the view.

For a moment she just watched, mesmerised by the sheer volume of water that thundered over the precipitous edge of the rocky plateau and plunged into the river below, causing huge clouds of spray.

'It's amazing. Breathtaking.' The falls seemed to glow in the light and she felt Raul's arms tighten around her.

'*Garganta del Diablo*,' he murmured against her cheek. 'We call it the Devil's Throat. It is the largest cascade. I have arranged for a boat to take us up the Iguazú River tomorrow. You will love it.'

And she did.

It seemed that everything had been planned for her enjoyment and she felt as though she spent the entire time staring in wonder. And even in their suite in the hotel, she couldn't prise herself away from the balcony.

'I feel as though I have competition,' Raul drawled finally, hauling her back inside the suite and closing the door firmly. 'You're supposed to be looking at *me*, not the view.'

And the truth was, she couldn't stop looking at him. They ate dinner on their private terrace, away from other people and the sheer intimacy of their situation made the nerves jump in her stomach.

'Did you travel as a child?' He waited for the food to be served and dismissed the staff with a single movement of his arrogant dark head. 'Where did you go?'

'Nowhere in particular. Europe.' She selected a piece of fish and tried it. 'This is delicious. We just went on normal family holidays. My parents would have loved it here,' she murmured, her eyes on the view as they lingered over dinner.

'You've told me virtually nothing about your childhood, but it was obviously very happy.'

'Why do you say that?'

He lifted his wine glass, a faint hint of mockery in his eyes. 'You have such a ridiculous faith in love and marriage that your parents must have been happy.'

And his hadn't been? She wanted to ask but she was afraid of spoiling the moment so instead she talked about herself.

'My parents met when they were teenagers and then Mum became pregnant with me.' Faith pulled a face. 'Terrible shock and scandal, because this was *years* ago and things were different then. My grandmother thought she was far too young but my father and mother were adamant that it didn't matter. "We're in love and we were always going to have a family at some point," my dad always said.'

And that, of course had been another reason why she hadn't questioned the motivations behind *their* own hasty marriage. She'd fallen in love with Raul. She couldn't imagine being with anyone else.

At first she'd been panicked that he wouldn't be pleased but when he'd immediately proposed she'd assumed that he'd adjusted to the idea as easily as she had.

'What you've just told me explains a great deal about you.' He sat across from her, his dark eyes fixed on her face, and she had the distinct impression that he was about to tell her something.

She sat still, willing him to offer up the confidence that she sensed hovered on his lips, but after a moment he rose to his feet and walked across to the rail that skirted the balcony.

Having learned not to press him to talk when he didn't want to, Faith resisted the temptation to prompt him and instead folded her napkin neatly and joined him by the rail. 'So where are we going tomorrow?'

He turned to face her, his dark eyes filled with secrets and shadows. Instead of answering her he took her face in his hands and kissed her with hungry, desperate urgency, his mouth hard and demanding on hers.

The kiss went from nothing to out of control in less time than it took him to back her into the suite and kick the door closed behind him. And after that there was no more talking.

CHAPTER ELEVEN

AFTER four glorious days and nights, they flew back to the *estancia* and Faith was feeling more settled.

The pregnancy might have triggered the marriage, but they were happy together, she knew they were.

The only slight blot on the landscape for her was that there were still moments when she didn't feel well physically, and that disappointed her because she could no longer attribute her lack of energy to the stress of their relationship or even lack of sleep. And it wasn't just that she was tired. Occasionally she was overwhelmed by dizziness and sickness and even though the doctor had assured her that such a reaction was quite normal after a head injury, she still felt uneasy.

But she didn't tell Raul because she knew that

if she so much as mentioned that she didn't feel well he would fly in an entire team of doctors from all over the world.

So she kept it to herself, hopeful that it would all fade in time.

They were happy together, and that was all that mattered.

'Raul's in a good mood because Pedro sold him the land!' Mateo, a business associate of Raul's, lifted his glass in a toast. 'And Raul is *always* in a good mood when he wins.'

They were dining in the most elegant restaurant in Buenos Aires, surrounded by the city's elite, their table giving them magnificent views over the vibrant city. Candles flickered on the tables and a jazz band played on the terrace outside.

'Raul *always* wins.' Julieta, Mateo's wife, glanced up from her plate. 'I thought you said he wanted to hang on to that land?'

'Apparently he wanted my money more,' Raul drawled, his long, strong fingers curled around the stem of his wine glass. 'I think he was influenced by my wife. Apparently I've become more human since I married her.'

'I wouldn't say so.' Mateo winked at Faith and

Julieta chuckled and reached across the table to take her husband's hand.

'Marriage is good for a man. It teaches him to share.' She frowned suddenly. 'You're quiet tonight, Faith. Are you all right? You're very pale. Raul, do you think she's pale?'

'She's English,' Mateo said cheerfully, leaning back as the waiter removed their plates. 'The English are always pale.'

'I'm fine.' Faith managed to smile, horribly aware of Raul's disturbingly intent gaze. The truth was that she felt *exhausted* and she just didn't understand the reason. Normally she was a very energetic person but at the moment she could have happily spent her life in bed. She just wanted to sleep and sleep.

It was probably just living with Raul, she concluded wryly. Too much sex. And she was worrying, of course, about where their relationship was going. Physically he was generous and demonstrative, but emotionally…

Reaching for her water, Faith took a sip. *Emotionally he still locked everything away.*

Julieta lifted her glass in a toast. 'To Emperor Raul, whose land now stretches across most of Argentina.'

Raul lifted an eyebrow. 'You're toasting me with water when there's champagne on offer?'

'Ah.' Julieta's eyes sparkled. 'We have news too, don't we Mateo?'

Mateo's expression softened. 'Julieta is pregnant. We found out yesterday.'

Faith felt as though all the air had been sucked out of the room. The noise and buzz of conversation around her faded to nothing and there was a rhythmic pounding in her ears.

For a moment she was enveloped in a blanket of panic and then she struggled free and realised that they were all looking at her expectantly, waiting for her to speak. 'That's fantastic,' she managed, genuinely pleased for Julieta and horrified by the vicious stab of jealousy that tore through her insides. 'We're so pleased for you, aren't we, Raul?' She answered for him because she didn't want him to say something tactless but deep down she wondered how he felt.

Of course, he wouldn't be as affected as she was, would he?

He didn't want children. She knew that. What she didn't know was why. And she wasn't likely ever to understand that because he didn't talk to her.

Faith struggled against the sudden surge of desolation that threatened to swamp her.

She wasn't going to think about her own situation. Not here. Not now in this public place in front of the man she loved and his friends.

But a thick, dangerous sludge of misery had been stirred inside her and refused to settle down.

She couldn't stop thinking about her own baby. The baby she'd lost.

An incredible sadness oozed through her and the lightness inside her faded away leaving only exhaustion.

In contrast, Julieta's face glowed with health and her eyes sparkled with excitement as she told them about her plans. Every now and then she touched Mateo's hand as if she couldn't quite believe that this was *her* life.

'It will be your turn next, Raul. Given that you've overcome your phobia of marriage, children are a logical next step.'

Worried that Raul might be upset, Faith intervened swiftly. 'It's too soon for that,' she said in a bright voice. 'I'm still hoping to pursue my career and we've barely spent any time together since we married.'

Trying to switch off her emotions, Faith concentrated on smiling, hoping that she looked more convincing than she felt because suddenly she was terrified she was going to break down. Right here. In public. With everyone watching.

What was the matter with her?

Why was she so tearful?

Over the past few weeks, all she seemed to do was sleep and it was completely unlike her.

'I'm delighted by your news, but you'll have to excuse us because Faith is very tired.' It was Raul who spoke and he rose to his feet in a decisive movement. 'It's time I took her home.'

For once Faith was relieved that he was so controlling and she shot the couple an apologetic smile. 'I don't think I'll ever become used to your Argentine hours—dining at eleven o'clock would be considered really odd in London.'

Julieta chuckled. 'That is a perfectly reasonable time in Buenos Aires. Are you seriously driving home? I thought you billionaires used a helicopter or a chauffeur.'

'I'm not good at being driven.' Raul strolled round the table, gently eased Faith to her feet and slid his arm round her waist. 'Great evening. We must do it again soon.'

Impossibly grateful that he'd rescued her, Faith

allowed him to guide her from the restaurant and into the low, sexy Ferrari that waited for them outside the door.

Determined not to cry, she slid into the passenger seat and closed her eyes. 'Thank you,' she muttered and heard the engine give a throaty roar as he pulled into the Buenos Aires traffic.

Raul glanced across at her but her eyes were closed and her face was pale.

Sleeping? Upset?

She definitely *had* been upset and he knew why, of course.

When Julieta had announced her pregnancy, the look on Faith's face had been one of utter desolation before her naturally generous nature had reasserted itself and she'd masked that response.

With a fluent oath, he flattened his foot to the floor, wishing that he *had* chosen to use the helicopter for this particular evening out in the capital.

He didn't like the fact that she was lying still and quiet next to him. He didn't even know if she was really asleep or just pretending. And either activity was completely unlike her. Before their wedding she'd possessed boundless energy and she'd wanted to talk about *everything*.

To his surprise he was fast discovering that her sudden silence disturbed him more than her emotional insights and probing questions.

At least when she'd done that he'd known how to respond.

Now he felt out of his depth and that was an *entirely* new feeling for him.

He was also worried that she was so pale and tired. Had she been pale before Julieta had made her announcement? His mind scanned the past. She'd been tired since her head injury and he frowned suddenly as he recalled the number of times he'd seen her curl up on the bed and fall asleep.

What if there was something wrong with her? *What if she was ill?*

He felt a sudden flash of foreboding.

Increasing his speed, he arrived at the *estancia* in record time but when he pulled into the court-yard, Faith still didn't wake. With a soft curse, Raul sprang from the car and threw his keys to a waiting member of staff. 'Call the doctor. I want him at the Beach House in the next ten minutes.'

'It's two in the morning—'

'I *know* what time it is.' Unaccustomed to having his orders questioned, Raul threw the man a warning glare. 'Just call him.' Then he strode round to the passenger side and scooped Faith into his arms.

Her head flopped against his shoulder and she stirred for a moment but didn't really wake up.

Trying not to think about how slender and impossibly fragile she was, Raul strode along the path into the Beach House and laid her on the bed.

Staring down at her, he hesitated for a moment and then bent down and gently pulled off her shoes. Deciding that the dress didn't look too comfortable either, he slid it down her body with the ease of experience and then wished he hadn't because she wasn't wearing a bra and her pale, rose-tipped breasts seemed to be crying out for his attention.

Teeth gritted, Raul grabbed the cover and pulled it over her semi-naked form, the unfamiliar degree of self-sacrifice leaving his body aching with raw sexual frustration. If this was how it felt to commit an unselfish act, he brooded, then he certainly wouldn't be making a habit of it.

As he tucked her in, Faith stirred and opened her eyes. 'Did I sleep all the way home? Sorry,' she murmured. 'Not very exciting for you.'

'I'm fine,' Raul lied smoothly, relieved to see that her cheeks had a little more colour. Perhaps she wasn't ill. She probably was just tired, he assured himself. After all, he wasn't allowing her much sleep at night, was he? And they were indulging in an unusual degree of physical activity.

And her mind was obviously working along the same lines because she gave him a slow, sleepy smile. 'Aren't you coming to bed?'

For a moment he was sorely tempted and then he remembered that the doctor would be arriving soon. To reduce the temptation to slide under the cover and bring some colour to her cheeks by alternative means, Raul retreated to the chair in the farthest corner of the bedroom. 'I'm not coming to bed yet.'

That statement was so out of character that it should have roused at least a question from Faith, but she simply looked at him. 'All right. Well, don't get too tired.'

Raul looked at her in exasperation.

Was that all she was going to say? What had happened to the probing and the questions? *What had happened to the talking?*

Feeling as though the whole situation was sliding out of his control, Raul decided to just give her the answer she hadn't asked for. 'I'm waiting for the doctor to come.'

'The doctor? Are you ill?' Her eyes widened and she sat up suddenly, her expression anxious.

'Not me,' he ground out, hastily averting his eyes from her breasts. 'You. I've called the doctor for you.'

'Why?'

'Because you're always tired.'

'I'm fine,' she began and he interrupted her with an impatient glance.

'You are *not* fine. You had a head injury and I want to know that these bouts of tiredness are a normal part of the recovery process.'

She looked at him with incredulity. 'It's the middle of the night, Raul!'

'I don't care,' he responded in a driven tone. 'I want a doctor to look at you.'

'I'm fine—'

'Stop saying you're fine. You're *not* fine. For a start you're not behaving like yourself.'

She pulled the covers up to her chin. 'I have no idea what you're talking about.'

Did he have to spell it out? He rose to his feet and ran his fingers through his hair. 'This evening—you were upset. About Julieta.' He saw the sudden wariness in her eyes and his mouth tightened. 'So why aren't you trying to talk about it? You *always* talk if something is upsetting you.'

'I thought I was supposed to phone a girlfriend for that.' Her tone was light and Raul tolerated the gentle dig because he was well aware that he deserved it.

He wasn't good at talking about things.

Even now he didn't want to have this conversation, but he knew he couldn't afford *not* to have it. 'I had no idea Julieta was pregnant,' he confessed in a raw tone. 'Or I would never have invited them to join us.'

'You can't protect me from everyone who is pregnant,' Faith said quietly and he gave a growl of frustration.

'That is *not* an answer. I want to know how you're feeling.'

'No, you don't, you know you don't. You *hate* it when I try and talk about feelings.' She brushed a strand of hair out of her eyes with a shaking hand. 'You just thought you ought to ask or I'll accuse you of not caring.'

His tension levels soaring through the roof, Raul removed his jacket and dropped it over the back of the nearest chair. 'I *do* care. The reason

I don't want to know is *not* because I don't care but because I feel guilty,' he confessed and a thick, heavy silence descended on the room.

Now she'd *have* to question him, he thought grimly and he stared at her in silent expectation, waiting for her to spill everything as she always did. Or probe him for how he felt.

She did neither. 'You have nothing to feel guilty about, Raul.'

'How can you say that?'

'Because it's true. As you once told me, you were completely up front about not wanting marriage or children. You're not to blame.'

He was about to respond when there was a knock on the door and two of his staff entered, accompanied by the doctor.

Raul dealt him a glance that would have flattened a man with fragile self-confidence, but the doctor stood his ground and nodded a greeting to Faith.

'I want you to find out what's wrong with her,' Raul commanded. 'And then I expect you to fix it.' Faith was young and supposedly healthy. It wasn't *normal* for anyone to be as tired as she was.

She no longer even had the energy to argue with him.

What if it was something serious?

Facing that terrifying prospect, a sudden chill of fear slid down his spine and he glared at the doctor. 'Well? Aren't you going to examine her or something?'

'I certainly intend to examine her,' the doctor said calmly, walking across to the bed and placing his bag on the floor.

'Well hurry up then.' Raul's voice was hoarse and the doctor sighed.

'If you would leave us alone for a few moments, I'd like to talk to your wife.'

'Leave you alone?'

'Yes.' The doctor opened his bag and removed a stethoscope. 'I insist that all my consultations are private in the first instance. Later, if your wife chooses to have you in the room, we can call you.'

Raul opened his mouth to refuse but then re-membered that Faith had completely clammed up with him. He knew her well enough to know she needed to talk to *someone* and since it wasn't him, then it had better be the doctor.

Prepared to make that sacrifice for the greater good of their relationship, Raul turned and left the Beach House in several long, angry strides.

'Your husband seems very tense and worried,'

the doctor observed, checking Faith's temperature and her pulse rate. 'He obviously loves you very much.'

If only. Faith decided that it was best not to respond to that statement because she didn't trust herself not to break down and sob. In a state of anxious misery, she lay still while the doctor examined her but all she really wanted to do was run after Raul.

They'd been in the middle of a conversation about Julieta's pregnancy when the doctor had arrived and for some reason he'd been getting more and more exasperated with her.

She'd done her best not to cry on him or talk about the way she felt because she knew he *hated* that, but instead of appearing relieved and grateful for her restraint, he'd actually seemed more agitated.

This whole thing was her fault. If she'd told him that she'd lost the baby before the wedding then he never would have married her. Maybe they wouldn't even be together.

Finding that scenario deeply depressing, Faith closed her eyes tightly and it took her a moment to realise that the doctor was speaking to her.

'Sorry. Did you say something?'

'I asked you when your last period was.'

Faith gave him the date. 'Why are you asking? What does that have to do with my head injury?'

'Because I don't think your symptoms are anything to do with your head injury,' the doctor mused, folding his stethoscope and putting it back into his bag. 'I have a suspicion this is something entirely different.'

'Well it must be something,' Faith muttered. 'Because I'm completely exhausted and that isn't like me.'

'It's definitely something,' the doctor said mildly. 'When was your last period?'

Faith gritted her teeth. 'I haven't had one since the miscarriage.'

'And when was the miscarriage?'

She gave the doctor the date and then turned her head away. 'Do we really have to talk about this?'

'If you're asking whether it's important then the answer is yes, I think it is.' The doctor sat down next to her, his expression thoughtful. 'This miscarriage—describe it.'

So Faith told him what had happened and he gave a slow nod.

'And you didn't see a doctor?'

'No. It was very early on so I didn't see the point. What could anyone have done?' Feeling the emotion bubbling up inside her, she covered her face with her hands. 'Can we stop talking about this? Why is it even relevant?'

'Because I don't think you lost that baby,' the doctor said in a calm, clear voice. 'In fact I'm entirely sure that you're still pregnant.'

His words were so entirely unexpected that Faith lay still, just staring at him. 'S-still pregnant?'

'You had a small bleed at the time that your period was due. It happens. Far more frequently than people imagine, actually. It wasn't a miscarriage. By my calculation you're about three months pregnant.'

Pregnant?

She hadn't lost the baby?

Her hand covered her flat stomach in an instinctively protective gesture and a rush of pure, perfect joy engulfed her.

And then the implications of what the doctor had just told her sank into her brain and she immediately swooped down into a dark pit of despair.

The fact that she hadn't lost the baby was wonderful news, but she realised with a miserable, sinking heart that the doctor's words had sounded the death knell for her relationship with Raul.

* * *

Faith walked onto the beach, bracing herself for the most difficult conversation of her life.

How would Raul respond to the news?

He wouldn't be pleased, she knew that. Suddenly his comment on her wedding day came back to haunt her.

Although it was four in the morning, there was just enough light for her to make out his lean, powerful physique. He stood with his back to her, facing out to sea, and she lifted a hand to touch him and then immediately let it fall again.

What right did she have to touch?

'Raul?' She spoke his name softly and he turned instantly.

The sudden flare of anxiety in his eyes surprised her. 'Well?' He reached out and put his hands on her shoulders, his hard, strong fingers biting into her flesh. *'What did he say?'*

Faith flinched. 'You're squeezing me—'

'Sorry.' He released his grip and took her face in his hands, stroking her cheeks with his thumbs. 'I'm sorry, *cariño*. I've been worried.'

The concern in his tone almost finished her off. 'I'm sorry you were worried.' How was she going to say this? What words could she use to make the whole thing easier on both of them? 'I—Raul—'

'*Dios mío*, you're scaring me,' he said hoarsely. 'Just tell me, quickly, before I chase after that damn doctor and drag him back here. What did he say to you that's made you so scared? You look totally terrified! Whatever it is, we'll fix it, I promise.'

It was such a typical response that in spite of her misery, she almost smiled. 'You can't fix everything, Raul.' Feeling as though she were facing a firing squad, Faith moved her face away from his hands and stepped back from him but still she couldn't bring herself to say what had to be said because she knew that once the words were out there, that would be it.

Their relationship would be over.

Her fingers were trembling, her legs were trembling—she felt physically sick although whether that was down to nerves or her pregnancy she didn't know.

Squeezing her eyes shut she vowed that, whatever he said, she was *not* going to cry. Inside she felt wretched, miserable and just plain desolate.

'Faith,' Raul muttered rawly, turning her to face him. 'If you don't tell me soon—'

She tilted her head back and braced herself. What difference did a few minutes make? She wanted a whole lifetime with him and if she couldn't have that...

'I'm pregnant.' Her voice cracked and she snatched a breath and said it again, just in case he hadn't heard her. 'I didn't lose the baby. I made a mistake about that. I'm still pregnant.'

He stared down at her, his dark eyes glittering in the moonlight and his normally bronzed, healthy skin appeared to have lost some of its colour.

His hands dropped from her arms and he took a step backwards, an expression of stunned disbelief crossing his handsome face.

He didn't say a word.

Not a single word.

The only sound was the soft rush of waves as they broke onto the sand and the frantic pumping of her own heartbeat.

Raul stared down at her for what seemed like endless minutes and then turned sharply and walked away across the sand.

And that, she thought to herself, was that.

No longer bothering to contain the tears that had gathered in her throat, Faith sank down onto the sand and just sobbed.

CHAPTER TWELVE

PACKING was easy because she didn't need to take much.

Just her work gear and a suit that she thought she could use for interviews. The glamorous shoes and dresses she ignored because she just couldn't imagine herself ever wanting to party again.

Closing the small case, she carried it over to the door of the Beach House and then turned to allow herself one last look. Four large, stylish lamps threw shafts of golden light across the room and for one desperately indulgent moment she stood, gazing at the pale wood floors, the filmy white curtains and the soft sofas piled with exotically coloured cushions.

It was just a house, she reminded herself bleakly. *Just a house.*

If she wanted to, she could reproduce it in the next place she lived.

Except that it wasn't just a house, was it?

Everything about the place reminded her of Raul. *It had been their home.*

She turned off three of the lights and was just reaching to do the same with the fourth, when Raul's voice came from behind her.

'If you seriously think I'd let you walk away from me a second time then you don't know me at all.' His words shimmering with suppressed violence, he spoke from the doorway and Faith turned, her heart rate suddenly doubling.

'I thought you'd—' She stumbled over the words. 'I thought you'd gone.'

'Gone?' Winged dark brows met in a menacing frown. The collar of his shirt was undone and his eyes blazed dark with anger. 'Gone where?'

'I don't know.' Her legs were trembling and her stomach was churning and she gave a helpless little shrug. 'As far away as possible, I suppose.'

The last remaining light illuminated his black, glossy hair and the fierce burn of his eyes. 'I'm not the one who runs in this relationship. Does our marriage really mean so little to you?' His tone grim, he strode forward and took her face in his hands, forcing her to look at him. 'If you're going to cry, you can damn well cry on my shoulder. Not on some stranger in an aeroplane.'

'This isn't the time to be possessive and territorial,' she muttered in a thickened voice. 'Just let me go, Raul.'

His answer to that was to slide an arm around her waist, locking her against him. 'Talk to me, *cariño*. I want to know what you're thinking because at the moment the working of your brain is a complete mystery to me and I'm not used to that. Usually you talk about *everything*. Why would you even consider leaving when we are so good together?'

'Didn't you hear what I told you? I'm pregnant.'

His eyes narrowed warily. '*Sí*, I heard that part. What I didn't hear is why this news would make you miserable. I thought you *wanted* this baby.'

'I did. I do.' She gave a painful little smile. 'But I also wanted you and the two things aren't compatible are they? You don't want babies. *You don't like children!*'

Her passionate statement was met by a long throbbing silence and then he drew in a long breath and released her, his shoulders tense and his eyes suddenly wary. 'I have never *once* in our relationship told you that I don't like children.'

'No marriage, no babies.' Her tone was flat as she quoted him word for word. 'That's what you told me.'

'Perhaps. I mean—' For some reason his English seemed to lack its usual fluency. 'Yes. I *did* say that but I have never said that I didn't *like* children.' He ran a hand around the back of his neck and his obvious struggle to find the words he wanted puzzled her. She'd never known Raul anything less than stunningly articulate.

'It's fine, Raul. You honestly don't have to explain.'

'*Dios mío*, I am *trying* to tell you something. Usually you are pushing me and pushing me to talk and talk and suddenly when I am trying to talk, you are stopping me!' His fierce glare suggested that he was holding her personally responsible for his difficulties in that area and her eyes widened.

'Because I know you hate talking—'

'I *want* to tell you.'

'Oh.' Her heart thudding, she looked at him expectantly and his eyes darkened angrily.

'I have no idea how to say it,' he snapped at her impatiently. 'I'm not *like* you. I can't just spill out everything I'm feeling. I've never actually said this before so I have no idea how to say it.'

Faith waited patiently and he glared at her again.

'It isn't that I don't *like* children,' he began, but then he stopped, a frown on his face.

Faith decided that she'd better help him. 'I understand. You have this great life, Raul.' She waved an arm in the vague direction of the *estancia*. 'You fly off in your private jet at a moment's notice, you can dine in Paris or New York whenever you like without giving another thought to another person. Why would you want to compromise that lifestyle?'

Raul left a long pause before he answered.

'It wasn't Sofia.'

His driven, emotional statement seemed unrelated to the conversation they were having and for a moment she just stared at him, scanning her mental frequencies for clues. 'What wasn't?'

'Sofia wasn't the reason I'm reluctant to have children,' Raul confessed with raw emphasis. 'It happened long before her.'

Faith stood completely still. 'But it was a woman who hurt you?'

'Yes, but not in the way you're imagining.' He stood for a moment, his breathing slow and steady, as if he were concentrating on that one action. A tiny muscle flickered in his hard jaw and it was several long seconds before he spoke again. 'She took away *everything* that mattered to me, *everything* I loved. She was vicious, selfish and greedy.'

A deafening silence followed his hoarse statement and for a moment Faith was afraid even to move. She *felt* his agony but she suppressed the natural instinct to offer comfort, sensing that if she said the wrong thing now, he'd retreat. So she stood for a moment with her head full of words but her mouth tightly shut.

He glanced towards her and his eyes locked with hers. 'I promised myself, never again. Never would that happen to me.'

Faith had to force herself to ask the question. 'Was she someone that you loved?'

His dark eyes glinted hard and cold and his mouth tightened to a thin line. 'She was my mother.'

His confession was such a shock that for a moment Faith couldn't respond.

Of all the scenarios she'd imagined, that hadn't been one of them.

Clearly he wasn't surprised by her inability to

speak, because he grimaced. 'Not every woman is maternal. She became pregnant to force my father into marriage. No other reason. They divorced when I was nine and it was *extremely* acrimonious. She was determined to take my father for every penny he had and I was the tool she used to do it. And once she'd stripped him bare of everything that mattered, she took me, too.'

'You mean you stayed with your mother?'

His eyes glittered dark and dangerous. 'I mean that she took me from him. Not because she loved me or wanted me, but because she knew how much my father did. I was her trump card.'

Shocked, Faith shook her head in disbelief. 'No.'

'This was my father's land.' Raul turned, looking through the windows of the Beach House towards the *estancia*. 'He was a horseman. A very skilled horseman. There wasn't a horse in South America that my father couldn't work with. He had more patience than any man I've ever met.' He glanced at Faith, his eyes gleaming with self-mockery. 'Needless to say, I have my mother's genes. She was volatile and explosive, given to *major* tantrums.'

'I didn't know your father owned the *estancia*. I thought you bought it.'

'I did. It was sold after the divorce. My father gave my mother the money because he couldn't bear to think that I might suffer. Even though this place had been in my family for generations, he sold it.' Raul was silent for a moment, emotion radiating from every angle of his powerful frame. 'So that's what she did. On the other side of the world.'

'Estancia La Lucia,' she murmured softly. 'I never even asked you about the name. I—'

'Lucia was my great-great-grandmother.'

She'd had no idea. 'Raul—'

'This *estancia* had been our family's heritage for more than a hundred years. It was in my father's blood and in my blood.' Raul's voice was rough. 'He taught me to ride before I could walk. We were going to run this place together.'

Faith stood in silence, absorbing his horrible, horrible story, her insides aching as she imagined the pain of that little boy, longing for his father. 'You couldn't stay with him?'

'A child stays with his mother. That's the tradition isn't it? She told me we were going on holiday.' Each word was another beat of agony. 'It was only when we arrived in Australia that she told me that we wouldn't be coming back.'

Faith licked dry lips. 'You must have missed him so much.' She put her hand on his arm and felt the flex of his strong muscle and the utter chill of his skin.

'At first I refused to accept it. I ran away. I made it as far as the airport and then they rang my mother.' He gave a dark, cynical smile that revealed far more about that encounter than any words could have. 'And she told me to grow up and be a man. And that's what I did. Every day I was in hell, but I kept that hell to myself and just lived it. I was trapped in an alien country with people who were alien to me. I pined for my father, for Argentina, the *estancia*, the horses—everything. I hated the life my mother led and the fact that she didn't even want me. But I learned not to show what I was feeling.'

'And you still don't—'

His beautiful mouth twisted. 'I think I've forgotten how.'

'But you left Australia?'

'I left as soon as I could and came back here only to find that my father had sold the *estancia* to pay for my mother's costs. It was broken up and sold.' His accent grew more pronounced. 'He was trying to make sure that I had a good life. That I didn't suffer. But for me it was never about the money.'

Touched by this surprisingly emotional admission, Faith leaned forward and wrapped her arms around him. 'So you started your own business. What you have achieved is nothing short of amazing.'

'I vowed to buy it back, piece by piece. And I have.'

'The land that Pedro owns…'

'*My* land now.' His possessive declaration vibrated around the room. 'That was the last piece. My father's *estancia* is back in the family again.'

'And your father?' She felt the muscles in his body tighten and suddenly wished she hadn't asked the question.

'After my father sold the *estancia*, he took a job as a *gaucho*—a cowboy—working with horses on other ranches. I know, because I followed his trail. He kept moving on, restless.'

'He didn't make a home anywhere else?'

'He never would have done that because his home was here. He died,' Raul said roughly. 'He died without knowing that I was back. He died before I made my first million and purchased the first thousand acres of land.'

And he'd died without giving his son the chance to tell him how much he loved him.

'You say that there is nothing of your father in you, but I don't think that's true,' Faith said softly. 'You have his strength and his courage, his talent with horses and his love for this land.'

He looked down at her, his eyes fierce. 'What my mother must have put him through—' he said hoarsely. 'I swore that no woman would ever be able to do that to me or to any child of mine.'

For a moment Faith couldn't speak because she couldn't get the words past the lump in her throat. 'So it isn't that you don't like or don't want,' she said softly. 'It's that you're afraid of loving and losing. Now I understand why you married me. You were determined to do everything possible to exert your rights over the baby.'

'Faith—'

'And I don't blame you for that. If I'd been through what you have, I'd feel the same way, I'm sure.' Faith stood still, thinking about what he'd said. 'I wish you'd told me this, instead of just proposing. I would have understood.'

'You would have run a mile, taking my baby with you.' It was the most painfully honest conversation they'd ever had. 'And you did run,

Faith. Just hours after you married me, you ran. That's what women do when things go wrong. That's what my mother did.'

She bit her lip, understanding why her actions had triggered such a depth of emotion in him. 'That's true,' she admitted, 'I did. But you have to look at it from my point of view. When I told you I lost the baby you were *relieved*.'

'I hadn't expected to have to confront the issue of pregnancy at all. For me it was simpler if it just wasn't there.'

'I see that now, Raul, but at the time you hadn't shared any of this with me. All I saw was a man who was so fixated on his own desire to stay single that he didn't care about my feelings. You thought I'd become pregnant on purpose.'

'Which was exactly what my mother did. And I wasn't thinking about your feelings. I was thinking about mine,' he grated. 'Panicking. I know I hurt you and I regret that more than you know. I was a total bastard, but it wasn't anything to do with you—I was protecting myself.'

'Because you thought I'd hurt you?'

'You have to understand that none of my relationships up until now have ever been based on anything other than sex,' he confessed and she

looked up at him, her heart executing a dangerously fast rhythm.

'And now?'

'You really need to ask that? It's true that I'm
totally out of control when I'm with you, *cariño*,
but believe me when I tell you it isn't just about
the sex. I love the fact that you're so bright and
clever, I love the fact that everything in your
head comes out of your mouth because it makes
you so easy to understand.'

Faith was astonished. 'You hate the fact that I
want to talk!'

'*Not* true,' he asserted, bending his head and
stealing a quick kiss. 'In fact since you stopped
talking, it's driven me mad because I'm wasting
so much time guessing what's in your head.'

Her legs wobbling, Faith sank down onto the
nearest sofa. 'This is—' She broke off and
breathed in and out. 'This isn't the way I thought
this conversation would go. When you walked
away from me—I assumed you were horrified
that I was still pregnant.'

'I went to talk to the doctor. I'd managed to
convince myself that there was something really
wrong with you. You were so pale and tired—I
wanted to make sure he'd taken a really good

look at you,' Raul confessed. 'I'm not great at trusting other people with important issues. I virtually pinned him to the wall and made him recite everything he'd told you.'

Knowing Raul as she did, Faith had no problems imagining it. 'And how did he respond to that?'

'He wasn't that impressed,' Raul admitted wryly. 'But he told me he was making allowances for a guy who was seriously in love.'

His words drove the air from her lungs. 'He did? And did you tell him you don't believe in love?'

'No, because that wouldn't have been true.' He reached for her hands and pulled her back to her feet. 'I *didn't* believe in love, until I met you. And even then I didn't recognise it. But apparently the signs are all over the place if you know what you're looking for.'

Her heart pounding, Faith looked up at him. 'Is that right?'

'Of course.' His usual confidence apparently restored, Raul curved his arms around her in an unmistakably possessive gesture. 'I can't let you out of my sight, I worry if you're even half a shade paler than you usually are and when you stop wanting to talk about everything I get really, *really* worried.'

'You *hate* talking.'

'Given a choice between conversation and sex, I'm going to pick sex every time,' Raul admitted, with typical male frankness. 'But I'm prepared to concede that a certain degree of emotional honesty has its place.'

'Does it?'

'Yes.' He smoothed her hair away from her face. 'I should have talked to you sooner, but you have to understand that I've never talked to *anyone* about this. I don't even let myself think about it.'

'I don't blame you, but I'm glad I know because now I can understand why you feel the way you do. And I have something to say that's important.' Faith took a deep breath. 'You don't have to stay with me just because you're afraid of losing your child, Raul. I would never take your child from you, ever. If you're saying this because of the baby, then we can work something out. You own ten-thousand acres—you can build me a house to live in.'

'I am not building you a house to live in. The only place you're living is here with me,' he growled and Faith bit her lip.

'I'm worried, Raul,' she said quietly. 'I'm worried that you're only saying this because of the baby. I mean, it's not as if you had a choice about this.'

'Come with me!' Having delivered that command, he took her hand and led her up the staircase to the upper floor.

'Where are we going? We never come up here—' Exasperated, she tugged at his hand. 'Raul, we were *talking*—'

'And talking is fine,' he purred, turning to her with his most charismatic smile. 'But there are times when actions speak louder than words, *cariño*.'

Mesmerised by that incredibly sexy smile, Faith felt her insides tumble and flip and gave a moan of disbelief. No, no, no! She wasn't going to respond like this, not now! They were discussing an important issue. *Surely* he wasn't going to try and solve this problem with sex? Not after the discussion they'd just had. 'Raul, this just isn't—'

'Trust me.' With his usual confidence, he threw open a door and stepped aside for her to pass him. 'Go in. Tell me what you see.'

Puzzled, Faith stepped inside the room and her heart tumbled over in her chest.

It was a nursery.

A beautifully decorated, sunny nursery complete with an old-fashioned rocking chair, an antique cot and pretty curtains.

For a moment Faith couldn't speak at all and then when she finally tried to say something, nothing came out of her mouth.

His hands curved over her shoulders. 'What do you see?'

'I see—' Her voice cracked. 'I see a nursery.'

'No.' He gently turned her and cupped her face in his hands. 'You see a man in love.'

'But—'

Raul was watching her reaction with a self-satisfied smile on his handsome face. '*Now* try telling me I'm insensitive,' he drawled softly, pulling her against him and bringing his mouth down on hers. 'I had this decorated when we were on our honeymoon.'

'Our honeymoon?'

'That was when I realised that I couldn't imagine a life without you in it. I didn't know you were still pregnant, Faith. But this was how I saw our future. As a family.'

She felt tears prick her eyes. 'You—you'd already done this?'

His eyes gleamed with sardonic humour. 'You

think I shot up here with a paint brush five minutes after the doctor left?'

'No. Yes.' Tears filled her eyes and his smile faded.

'Don't cry. *Te amo, cariño*. I love you. Do you understand me?' He took her face in his hands and kissed her gently. 'Do you? Answer me, because if you don't then I will have to solve the problem the way you suspected I was going to solve it.'

She sniffed and made a sound that was half sob, half laugh. 'I thought—'

'I know what you thought and perhaps that would have been a better option.' He frowned. 'Given that talking just seems to make you cry.'

'I thought I was going to lose you. I know you only married me because I was pregnant.'

'I married you because you were pregnant,' Raul agreed in a husky tone. 'But I'm *staying* married to you because I love you.'

She squeezed her eyes shut but the tears fell anyway because she just adored him so much and suddenly everything had gone from being wrong to being very, very right. 'I love you, too. So much. You have *no* idea.'

'I think I have.' His voice was soft and he brushed the tears away from her cheek with the back of his hand. 'I behaved so badly to you. I was cruel and thoughtless and yet you are still here. You have to be in love to have put up with me. Stop crying!'

'I can't,' she croaked. 'And it's your fault. It's all the things you're saying.'

'Which just goes to prove that talking has its limitations,' he drawled, a dangerous gleam in his eyes as he lowered his head to hers. 'So now it's time to solve this problem in a very different way. Do you agree?'

'Yes,' Faith whispered against his mouth. 'Oh yes.'

MILLS & BOON PUBLISH EIGHT LARGE PRINT TITLES A MONTH. THESE ARE THE EIGHT TITLES FOR FEBRUARY 2009.

❧

VIRGIN FOR THE BILLIONAIRE'S TAKING
Penny Jordan

PURCHASED: HIS PERFECT WIFE
Helen Bianchin

THE VÁSQUEZ MISTRESS
Sarah Morgan

AT THE SHEIKH'S BIDDING
Chantelle Shaw

BRIDE AT BRIAR'S RIDGE
Margaret Way

LAST-MINUTE PROPOSAL
Jessica Hart

THE SINGLE MUM AND THE TYCOON
Caroline Anderson

FOUND: HIS ROYAL BABY
Raye Morgan

MILLS & BOON PUBLISH EIGHT LARGE PRINT TITLES A MONTH. THESE ARE THE EIGHT TITLES FOR MARCH 2009.

❧

RUTHLESSLY BEDDED BY THE ITALIAN BILLIONAIRE
Emma Darcy

MENDEZ'S MISTRESS
Anne Mather

RAFAEL'S SUITABLE BRIDE
Cathy Williams

DESERT PRINCE, DEFIANT VIRGIN
Kim Lawrence

WEDDED IN A WHIRLWIND
Liz Fielding

BLIND DATE WITH THE BOSS
Barbara Hannay

THE TYCOON'S CHRISTMAS PROPOSAL
Jackie Braun

CHRISTMAS WISHES, MISTLETOE KISSES
Fiona Harper

MILLS & BOON®
Pure reading pleasure™